A LOVE UNREFINED

IVY LAIKA

B. LOVE PUBLICATIONS

INTRODUCTION

This is a spin-off of Untainted Love. It can be read as a standalone, but I recommend reading Untainted Love first to better understand the dynamics of the characters.

Let me first thank everyone for their continued support. My name is Ivy Laika, but many don't know that it's pronounced Evie Lah-EE-kah. (The I is pronounced E in Haitian Creole)

When I wrote my first book, Untainted Love, my goal was to write a book and possibly get it published. I didn't even think about writing a second one. But thanks to the unwavering support of my best friend, here I am at book three. It feels surreal and because of that, book three is dedicated to you.

To my readers new and newer, my goal with all my books is to create organic chemistry between the main characters. I want readers to feel how they felt in that moment. I want readers to crave for a love like theirs and realize that type of love is out there. No pressure just let everything happen, how it's supposed to happen, when it's supposed to happen.

I am Haitian so there will always be a part of my culture sprinkled in all my books. My hope for that is that you get to know more about other African Diasporas because even though we are different we do share some similarities. My culture has molded my perspective on life and I want to be able to share that with all of you.

Lastly, I hope you all enjoy A Love Unrefined. I strived for this book to be a bit different. If you would like to stay connected with me or my work, please follow me on IG and FB under Ivy Laika. You can also request to join my FB group: Laika's Love Lounge.

Once again, thank you for downloading my book. Enjoy and please leave a review

Signed,
   Ivy Laika- Lover of love. Nurturer of souls

CHAPTER 1

*S*aint

"How you are feeling, bro?"

"Real good but marriage isn't easy. I honestly can't believe it's really been a year since Ladi said yes to becoming my wife," my younger brother, Ace, responded.

He and my sister-in-law, Ladi, were celebrating their one-year wedding anniversary in their backyard. The same place where they exchanged their vows a year ago. Seeing that he found the love and happiness that he had been searching for, was refreshing because he dealt with some trifling females in the past. I could've thrown a party when he finally decided to cut his ex, Sasha, off. She was the worst type of woman. God only knew how much I wanted to beat his ass for dating her in the first place. It blew my mind how our mom gave him the perfect example of what a great woman was, but he chose to waste his time on Crazy Ass Sasha. Next to her, there was my wife, Angel. She embodied the hell out of her name. How he even thought Sasha was an ounce of those two women was beyond me.

"Marriage was never meant to be easy but I'm proud of

you. Especially for letting that scandalous girl go." I hit my balled-up fist on the round table that was covered with a white linen cloth, before laughing loudly. The music that was playing covered up my laughter, so none of their thirty-something guests turned to look in our direction. The guest list consisted mostly of our family members, a few of their employees that they regarded as close associates, and my general manager, Ashley. Her, Angel, and Ladi had became a tight group over the past year.

"I swear I can't stand you bro," he said as he rubbed his hand down his face. It was his way of calming himself down from getting irritated.

"Me, nigga?" If it was up to me, Sasha wouldn't have made it past date one with him. I continued, "Was I the one that introduced you to her? Nah, say you can't stand yourself."

Having messed with him enough for the night, I got myself together before leaving him at the table alone to go find me wife. My mom was in town and agreed to watch our three children, so that we could go to a hotel for the night for some overdue alone time. I loved all three of my kids but shit, we needed our alone time too.

I found Angel in the kitchen helping Ladi set the food up to be served. Ace wanted to get a caterer to handle everything but Ladi's aunt, Marie, refused. My mom cosigned with Auntie Marie, and consequently the two prepared all the food while Ladi and Angel set everything up. I strolled up behind my beautiful wife and wrapped my arms around her waist. Her head fell to my chest as I held her securely. The woman was everything to me. I loved every inch of her. Angel's hair was cut into a pixie cut that she had recently dyed honey brown. Her size fourteen frame was draped nicely in a white knee length, off-shoulder bondage dress.

Yeah, I had me a full-figured woman. She had lost some weight after having our youngest child, Miracle, but she hadn't lose any of the curves that I loved.

She whimpered softly as I pressed myself on her round ass. "Don't get nothing started babe," I whispered in her ear.

"Please, not over the food," Ladi said, turning her face up. It didn't bother me any because I was going to show my wife affection no matter where we were or who was around. Anyone that had a problem with it would just have to deal with it. Both Angel and I knew that Ladi was joking around.

"Does anybody tell you and Ace anything when ya'll be all over each other?" I asked.

She offered me a side smirk before saying, "Don't worry about what we do."

I was almost positive that she was going to tell Ace what I said about them. She finished up setting up the food before going outside. Once she was out of the door, I turned my attention back to my wife.

"You must be ready for baby number four dressed like that babe." Angel let out a soft sigh and I immediately regretted mentioning another baby.

Angel and I suffered a couple of miscarriages after having our soon-to-be four-years-old twins, Heaven and Saint Jr, SJ. A year and a half ago, she gave birth to our little miracle. Naming that little girl Miracle was only fitting. We both had been hurting from the possibility of Angel not being able to conceive after having surgery to get one of her ovaries removed when the twins were born. It rocked me but I tried my best to remain strong for her.

It wouldn't have been fair to her for me to shed my tears in front of her. It wouldn't have been fair for me to have my emotional breakdowns while she was battling depression. I kept it all in until I went to work. When I was alone in my office, then and only then would I let everything out. Only Ace knew about them and that was only because he walked in on me once. Her having Miracle was just what we needed. Our love was unmatched because it was a love that came after trust. But the family that we created, that was our glue. Angel knew I wanted more children, but I had never verbally expressed it until now. Now that Miracle was one and a half, it was the perfect time to try again. Yes, we ran the risk of her having another miscarriage but the possibility of being able to extend our family outweighed all of that.

She didn't say anything in response, instead she simply stared at me with her dark brown doe-shaped eyes before giving me a tender kiss on the lips. That gesture was my sign that she didn't want to talk about it. She'd been doing that since we met ten years ago. She was eighteen years old, while I was twenty-five. My heart didn't care about the age difference. It saw past her troubled past and her being seven years younger than me. It saw Angel for who she truly was, a beautiful soul.

"Let's go back outside baby. It's almost time for Ace to make his toast to Ladi." She wrapped her hand around mine and led me back into the backyard, just in time to witness Ace begin his speech.

"I'd like to thank everyone for coming and celebrating mine and Ladi's union. Marriage isn't for the weak but there isn't another woman--dead or alive--that I want to go through this journey with. Thank you for becoming my better half when I didn't realize a part of me was missing. Here is to one year and more importantly, to our forever."

He sat the mic down on the round table in front of him and reached for Ladi's hand. She stood next to my brother; a whole foot shorter than him. Ace had always been a big ass nigga. Since we were younger, he had always been taller and bigger than me. I wasn't short at five-eleven, but I wasn't anywhere close to Ace's six-foot-three either.

After Ladi was on her feet, he handed her a champagne-filled flute to complete the toast. She didn't drink from it. He bent down to whisper something in her ear before he grabbed the microphone again. With the dumbest grin on his face he announced, "We were waiting until later to tell everyone. As you all can see, Ladi refused to drink the champagne that I made the mistake of offering. If you guessed the reason as to why she declined the champagne is that she's pregnant with our second child, then you are correct."

Everyone started cheering and clapping. My little brother was living the life he always wanted. I couldn't have been prouder in that moment. He had it all; a career, a thriving business, a lovely wife, a junior, and now he and his wife were about to welcome another life into the world. Yeah, I handed him the tools, but he became a man on his own. I wasn't a soft nigga by any means but seeing him like that did something to me.

Angel held onto my hand, causing me to look down at her standing five inches shorter than me. Her eyes told me that she was still processing the comment I made about us having another baby. As much as I had tried to make it come off as me being playful, she knew me well enough to know that there was more seriousness than anything to what I said. Truth was, I did want another baby with Angel. I was hoping she was ready to talk about it.

The rest of the night was a filled with liquor, dancing, and food. The Caribbean food and music created a great atmosphere to let loose. My wife and I danced all night. Angel did something for me that no other woman that I had been with in the past, could do. She made me become monogamous. And that's why we were in Ace's upstairs bathroom now with her bent over the sink and her dress hiked up to her waist. Her warmness drew me into my favorite place. My escape.

As I slid in and out of her slowly, her moans touched my ears in the sweetest melody. It was as if she hit the on button and I quickened my pace. Every time she moaned, I went deeper. With each whimper, I went harder. Angel didn't want to make love tonight, she wanted it rough. Like the good husband I had always been to her, I was going to oblige.

CHAPTER 2

*S*aint

Last night with Angel was exactly what I needed. We didn't want to leave the hotel when it was time to check out, but we had to. The kids were going spend the day with my mom so that Angel could have a girls' day with Ladi and Ashley. After dropping her off at our house in Coral Gables, I went to work. My wife having time to herself was one of my main priorities. As much as I loved spending time with her, I understood that she had to find ways to maintain her identity outside of our marriage and family.

She worked part time as a registered nurse at Jackson Memorial Hospital. She didn't have to work but again, she had to find ways to keep her identity outside of me and our three kids. She was a devoted wife and mother of three. She had a lot on her plate and as her husband, it was up to me to help her find her balance. I never wanted Angel to lose who she was within our marriage. She married me young. She was eighteen when we met and nineteen when we married.

Here's the thing, I didn't even know she was only eighteen when we first met.

I was born in Saint Lucia but was raised in Nashville, TN. Having lived most of my life there, I made a name for myself in the streets. My parents worked hard to take care of us, but I wanted more for all of us. When Ace got in accepted into Florida International State, I decided to move down to Florida with him. It was actually on one of my trips back home to Nashville that I met Angel. One of my friends was having a house party and he had invited me to it. Parties were never my thing. I was a 'drink at home with the people I trusted' type of person. But that one night, my second mind told me to go. By being in the streets, I knew the importance of listening to my intuition and energy. If something didn't feel all the way right, chances were, it wasn't. That night, nothing felt off.

The second I stepped foot into the house, my energy pushed me towards her. I say pushed because I literally tripped all over myself to get to close to her. She was there with her cousin, Harmony, who actually looked eighteen. From Angel's body to how she carried herself, nothing gave me the impression that she was that young. The conversation we had on the porch didn't give any inclination that she as young as she was. That same night, I invited her to have breakfast with me the following morning. I wasn't about to wait way until the next night to see her. She reluctantly accepted. By the end of our conversation on the porch, I had blocked and deleted every female in my phone that I had been dealing with at that time. Angel asked me my age when we sat down to eat, after which she pulled out her ID. She was in fact eighteen, so it was legal. I was definitely hesitant at first but since nothing felt wrong, I continued the date.

After our second date, I bought Angel an engagement ring. I didn't propose right then and there but that safe space that she provided me with that night, was proof that it was only a matter of time before our souls tied together.

The knock on my office door snapped me out of thoughts. I instructed whoever it was to come in. Ace's incredible hulk looking ass came trotting through it. He sat across from me before speaking, "You disappeared on us last night."

It was hard for me to keep a straight face. Right after Angel and I finished in the bathroom, she grabbed her purse and we were straight out the door. We left without saying goodbye to anyone.

"Yeah, we had to leave," I managed to say with a semi-straight face.

"Go ahead and let it out man," he said while shaking his head.

The laughter that erupted from my throat, led Ace to join me. "My bad for leaving without saying bye but you know how it is."

"Yeah, I do. It's cool. That's why I figured I'd come by and see you."

"Don't you have any meetings today? You know your big ass stays busy." I chuckled a little bit.

"I promise you, you're not as funny as you think you are bro."

I shook my head at him. "Stop hating man. That's the reason you're sitting there with that goofy ass smile holding your laugh in, damn near about to pass out. Laugh nigga."

He shook his head and let out a soft chortle. I continued, "Answer my question though. I figured you'd have a day full of meetings since you been off the last couple of days, preparing for last night's party."

"Ladi had a doctor's appointment today, so I'm starting back up tomorrow."

"Look man, congrats again on the new addition. I'm proud of you for real. How you are feeling?"

I really was proud of the man he had become. He wasn't the reason why I started hustling but he was definitely the reason I went as hard as I did before I retired five years ago. Hustling was how I built my parents two homes in Saint Lucia, so that they could live comfortably. It provided me the ability to pay Ace's way through undergrad and master's program. Hustling helped me start my chain of restaurant and lounges, Chez Saint. The streets were good to me, but they weren't friendly. At thirty, I walked away from that life and hadn't looked back since. Now at thirty-five years old, I had almost everything I wanted. Almost.

"I feel really good about it. This one was planned, unlike AJ. Ladi wanted AJ to have a sibling close in age since she never got that. She wants another boy, but I want a miniature version of her."

"You sure about that? Those little girls are something else Ace. I have two of them, so I'm an expert on how they have all the control even though they're so small."

"Positive. AJ is attached to her hip like superglue. I bet you that's the only reason she even wants another boy."

"SJ a mama's boy, too. I hate that shit. Do you think after this one, you'll have anymore?" My intentions for asking Ace that question was to get his advice on wanting another baby. He tended to be little more rational than I was at times. We favored some in appearance with our matching dark chocolate skin, full beards, and large masculine build. Other than that, we didn't look alike, and we didn't act anything alike majority of the time.

"We talked about it. She said in a couple of years we can try again."

"Would you be ok if she didn't want to have anymore though?" I questioned him.

"Damn, I never thought about that. Did Angel tell you something?" He sat up from the chair, with panic etched on his face.

"No, Angel didn't say anything." We both sat there in silence, waiting for the other to speak. Part of me already knew what he was going to say, and I wasn't ready to hear it.

"Then why are you asking all of these questions?"

"I want Angel and I to have another baby," I blurted out. Saying it out loud felt like I was releasing the weight of the world from my shoulders. He sat there while staring at me silently, forcing me to yell, "Say something nigga!"

"Are you ready for that?"

That was a dumb question if I ever heard one. Not biting my tongue, I made him aware of that. "That's a stupid ass question. Of course, I'm ready for another baby."

Angel and I were financially stable. We weren't multi-millionaire status, but the chain of Chez Saint restaurants and lounges brought in more than enough revenue for us to live way beyond what most people considered comfortable. The streets afforded me that. I was smart with my money. That was the one thing I would always keep from the streets: the hustler's mentality.

Making time for each one of my children individually was always at the top of my list of priorities, therefore I knew I had the time to dedicate to another one. Pulling back from work wasn't an issue. I had great managers in place at all locations since I fired the old manager, Chris, and replaced him with Ashley. He thought that Chez Saint meant Chez Chris, thus I had to let him go. I visited the other three locations once a month. Angel and the children always came along to turn it into a family vacation. Opening a Nashville location was in the works, but I was willing to postpone it in order to concentrate on building my family. So yeah, his question was stupid as hell to me.

"Let me elaborate on that. Are you ready for the possibility of losing that baby? Angel had what, two miscarriages? Are you ready for her to go through depression while you struggle to remain strong for her? Are you ready to have emotional break downs every day for a month again?"

I sat quietly, processing all the questions. Then I thought about the day Miracle was born and then answered, "Completing our family outweighs all of that."

CHAPTER 3

*a*ngel
  "When are you going to tell us about this new boo you have?" Ladi asked Chez Saint's general manager, Ashley.

Her and Ladi had been friends since Ladi first started working there as the assistant general manager a little over two years ago. She replaced Ladi when she went on maternity leave. Now that Ladi had her own restaurant to manage and Saint fired the old general manager, Ashley took over that position. She was twenty-five years old and easily one of the sweetest people I'd ever met. Her petite frame was similar to Ladi's and she wore her signature bright red box braids. Because of her and Ladi being close, her and I naturally became close as well.

"When I'm sure he's serious."

"Did he tell you he was serious?" I asked.

"Let me tell you two ladies something. Every man isn't Ace or Saint. There are some really good ones out there but there are a few bad ones too. The bad ones," she paused before continuing, "they lie. They are manipulative. They will feed you every dream only to leave you heartbroken in a pool of tears."

I listened to her while nodding my head. I knew exactly what type of men she was referring to. I dealt with my share of them before meeting Saint at a house party my cousin, Harmony, had dragged me to when I was eighteen. I hated to think of Saint as my savior but that was the only way to accurately describe him. He gave me a new life when he moved me to Florida after we dated for a few months. We saved each other the night we met. Nobody knew much of my past other than Saint and Harmony. I planned to keep it that way, too.

"I never experienced that, to be honest," Ladi said with a sad face. She looked at Ashley with so much compassion in her eyes. From what we knew about Ladi, she dated a couple men before meeting my brother-in-law, Ace, but it never went far. Ace was her first everything. When I tell you she fell hard, sis fell hard. I'm talking broken bones and all. I, on the hand, had experienced those type of men one too many times. To avoid opening up to her and Ashley, I occupied myself with my food.

"Consider yourself lucky," Ashley responded. "I like him but I'm watching for consistency and patterns."

"It's sad when you can't trust a person's words," Ladi said.

"Everyone doesn't see the value and power in the words they speak like you do Ladi," I finally spoke up. All three of us nodded our heads in agreeance.

We were having drinks and lunch at Ladi's restaurant. She had some of the best Haitian food in the city of Miami. Miracle had just stopped nursing and I was grateful because I needed a drink. Saint kept mentioning having another baby. It was stressing me out. He did it jokingly, but

I had been with that man for ten years, I recognized when he was being serious. I knew him well enough to see that his mind was set on us having another child.

Although I couldn't open up to the two about my past, I knew I could trust them with this information that I was about to drop on them. Other than Harmony, Ashley and Ladi were the only two I could share it with. That was saying a lot, considering the fact that I didn't even trust my best friend, Monica, with the information I was about to lay out for them.

I sat up in my seat after inhaling a deep breath. Rubbing my hands up and down my denim covered thighs, I released it. "I have something I need to talk to you guys about. Ladi you cannot take this information back to Ace. I'm not telling you to lie to your husband. What I am asking is that you do not share what I'm about to tell you with him. It's big y'all. Real big."

They both stared at me with wide eyes. Taking a sip of my Long Island Iced Tea I whispered, "I had the doctor tie my tubes after having Miracle."

The anticipation that was on their face quickly changed to confusion. Ashley responded first, "I don't get it."

"Saint wants another baby."

"Do you not want another baby?" Ladi asked.

"I do now, but it's not that simple," I replied.

I could see their minds racing, trying to figure out what I was trying to tell them. Finally, Ashley said, "I don't see what the issue is. You can get it reversed. All you have to do is tell Saint you will get it reversed when you're ready." She started back sipping on her glass of red wine, like it was as simple as she said it was. I wanted to knock the damn wine glass out her small ass hand. I didn't even know how she was able to guzzle that bitter shit down anyway.

"Let me start over. When I had the c-section to have Miracle, I had the doctor tie my tubes without Saint's knowledge."

They both gasped loudly, causing everyone that was in close proximity of us to look to where we were seated. Ashley rolled her eyes at them while Ladi quietly apologized by mouthing the word sorry. "Can ya'll chill, damn," I whispered after wolfing down the rest of my drink.

"Angel why did you do that without telling him? It's your body but I do think you should've told him that you were going to do it before you actually did it," Ladi stated.

"I don't know. Well, I do know but it doesn't make sense to me anymore."

"Why doesn't it make sense anymore?" Ashley asked before stuffing her face with the Haitian vegetable medley dish, legume. It amazed me how she ate more than I did but was barely one hundred and thirty pounds. If I smelled food for too long, I'd gain five pounds. Don't get me wrong, I loved my size and all of my curves. It just shocked me how she could eat as much as she did and not gain any weight.

"Ashley how do you eat as much as you do and not gain any weight?" I asked.

"Angel, focus!" Ladi snapped. I turned to face her. Ladi wasn't normally snappy, so it caught me off guard. "I'm sorry, I didn't mean to snap. But you obviously have been holding on to this for a long time. Now you're trying to deflect from it."

Shaking my head, I responded, "You're right. You are absolutely right. I am trying to deflect. Here's the thing, Saint and I always wanted to have four children. That was one of the things that we agreed on when we decided to start our family five years ago. After having the miscarriages and then finally having Miracle, I didn't think I could go through the pain of losing another one."

"Why didn't you tell him that? You don't think he would've been ok with it?" Ladi asked. She reached over and put her hands atop of mine. Ashley scooted her chair closer to me and wrapped her arm around my shoulder.

"He would've but me telling him that would mean that I was denying him of a chance to have another child, indefinitely. That would've broken him even if he understood why I wanted to do it. It was my way of protecting us from losing another one. Now that I've done it, I regret it. I want another baby and I want to give him another baby. Our babies are the constant reminders of our love."

"You can get it reversed," Ashley said. She was now rubbing her hand up and down my bare arm, trying her best to comfort me. I guess to keep me from crying but the only things that ever made me cry were my children. I hadn't cried years prior to having them.

"How am I going to explain a surgery to him?" I asked.

"Tell him that you're getting it reversed," Ashley stated.

"Then not only would I have to tell him I had my tubes tied without him knowing but I'd also have to tell him that I've been hiding it for over a year. Make that make sense." I wasn't trying to take my irritation out on her, but I didn't want to hear any of that.

"Angel, as some point you will have to tell him. Figure out when the best time is but do not let him find out another way. You've already told us. We aren't going to say anything, but you know that once information is out in the universe, it's only a matter of time before it spreads," Ladi said.

"You're right. Both of you are right. I'll tell him. It's just a matter of figuring out when and how."

We finished up lunch before going to get manicures and pedicures. That was one of the things that I loved most about Saint, he gave me time to just enjoy time to myself. It was not easy working, being a mother of three, and a wife to hot-headed Saint but he made sure to give me time away from each role.

I worked three days a week at Jackson Memorial Hospital because I wanted to. I didn't have to, but it was a way for me to have some type of independence outside of our marriage. Saint supported it completely. He was the one that paid my way through undergrad when I moved to Florida. Well, that along with another reason. He knew just how important it was for me to have that independence. Also, I took one or two days a week to spend time with my girls. The only time that was a problem was when I hung out with Monica. To simply put it, he hated her. She was the first real friend I made in Miami when I moved. Unfortunately, we had become distant after my birthday celebration two years ago. In fact, her and Ace dated for a little while. Nothing too serious but she felt as though she had something to prove when we all went on my birthday trip to Saint Lucia. Ladi and Ace were an item then and Monica had lost her freaking mind disrespecting her. Ladi was a better woman than me because being around Saint had turned me into a borderline hothead.

Since then, her and I spoke every once in a while, but it was evident she felt a certain way about Ladi and I becoming close. I had initially met Ladi years ago while attending Florida International University. We reconnected after her aunt had a seizure and I was the one that found her. I didn't even know she and Ace were dating then but Monica took it personal as if I was the one that set them up.

Because I knew better than to have Monica and Ladi

around each other, I was on my way to her house to visit her after hanging with Ladi and Ashley. She had texted me while I was getting my pedicure. Saint's mom had all three of the kids and Saint was going to pick them up when he was done at work. He was also cooking dinner tonight, so I didn't have to worry about any of that. It was probably going to be something simple, but his effort would not go unnoticed.

When I made it to Monica's house, she let me in, and we started to catch up on the weeks that passed without us talking. She had gotten a new job and was talking to a new guy. I couldn't have been happier. She knew better than to bring up Ace around me. She was my best friend, but Ace was my brother. By default, Ladi took precedence over her. That may have seemed harsh, but you would have to know the two to understand that. Ladi was family, she was my sister and it was family above all. She was also a better person than Monica. That's not to say Monica was a bad person, she just wasn't the best person. I looked past all of that to maintain our friendship.

We sat around and talked until it was seven in the evening when it was time for me to head home to my family. I enjoyed days when I was able to just be me, but the moments with them were the ones I cherished the most. They fulfilled me in more ways than one.

———

"Babe!" I yelled when I entered our five-bedroom house. It consisted of our master bedroom plus a room for each of the four children we originally planned on having. Saint had even gone to the extent of having a two-bedroom guest house built in the back yard after Miracle was born, to ensure no one would occupy the extra room when we had guests. I wasn't ready for his reaction to there may not ever being a fourth child, but eventually I would have to tell him.

"I'm in the kitchen baby!" he yelled back in his deep sensual voice. He was up to something. Saint was hotheaded jokester. That sensual voice only came out when he had something up his sleeve.

"Ooooo, my baby is fancy!" I teased him as I walked into the kitchen. He had two covered plates on the gray marble island that was in the center of our kitchen. He had pulled up two of the tall chairs from the bar for us to sit. There was a large bouquet of bright pink Hibiscus flowers in the middle of the island. The unofficial flower of my home. My real home.

"You know how your man does for his woman." He stood there shirtless with his dark chocolate skin beautifully inked with tattoos. His full shiny beard sat nicely on his handsome face. Saint's bald head, my goodness. His bald head was my favorite. I loved rubbing my hands on it when he would lay his head on my chest every night before we'd fall asleep. His gray sweatpants left little to nothing to the imagination. I didn't have to see it, feel it, or taste it to imagine it. I knew that part of him very well. He had rooted himself in me years ago and every time we made love, he made it a point to remind me just how much he had done so.

"Stop drooling over me baby. After you eat, you know I'll give you some," he said before chuckling.

"Shut it. Wasn't anybody drooling over your ugly self," I playfully sneered at him while waving my hands.

"Ugly where?" he asked before rubbing his beard, causing me to shake my head. Yeah, my husband was conceited as well. He had every reason to be. "Exactly. Now wipe your mouth before I put something in it that'll have you drooling more."

Just like that, he opened up the floodgate of my treasure box. He knew I loved when he talked like that. Saint was sweet and gentle with me most of the time but sometimes, I loved when he got nasty. Tonight, was one of those times.

"Don't make me go over there and pick you up. Come here," he said.

I may have been a size fourteen, but he picked me up with ease when I was a size sixteen. Him doing it now would have been nothing for him to do. Once I made it to the island, he pulled out my seat and helped me up to get situated. "What are we having for dinner? Tacos, burgers, or spaghetti? Did you feed my babies? Where are they?"

"First," he paused before bringing his soft lips to mine, "don't act like those are the only things I know how to cook."

He kissed me again, this time a second longer. "Second, don't play me like I wouldn't feed *our* babies."

Again, he planted another kiss on my lips and I was certain I was seeping through my jeans. He placed his right hand at my center. I opened my legs instinctively, allowing him access to press his hand up against her. "Lastly, they are in bed so that daddy can get some quality time with mommy tonight."

"So last night..." *Gasp.* "wasn't..." *Gasp.* "enough for you?" I managed to finally ask. He slowly rubbed on her as he nibbled on my neck.

"When has one night of you ever been enough for me, Angel?"

I closed my eyes as he slid his wet tongue up and down my neck. He was blessed between his thighs, but that tongue was a lethal weapon. A weapon that formed and prospered against me for the past ten years.

After he realized I wasn't going to respond, he said, "That's what I thought. Now hurry up and eat your spaghetti before it gets cold."

We both started laughing and I said, "Thank you for everything babe."

"You deserve it all baby."

CHAPTER 4

*a*ngel

Ten years I had been with this man and we never lost the passion. We didn't always see eye to eye, but our appetite for each other only intensified with the years. Waking up in the morning with a sore body, was proof of that. I opened my eyes to find my husband standing at our bedroom doorway with a tray of food in one hand, while using the other hand to hold Miracle in place on his left hip. She was my little chocolate drop. The twins favored Saint but had my light complexion. But Miracle, she was the splitting image of him and was closer to his dark complexion than she was to mine.

"What did I do to earn breakfast in bed?" I asked before sitting up. With my back against our cushioned headboard, I took my time to admire the stunningly sculpted specimen that was in front of me. He was rough around all of his edges but the love that he consistently showered me with, made me overlook his flaws. Marriage was hard but throughout the ten years that we had been together, there had never been any signs of infidelity. Not once was any woman ever able to approach me to claim any part of my man as hers. He protected me, provided fully, loved me, and gave me the family I never had. Saint was truthfully my saving grace.

"That's the least I could do after the things I did to you last night. I know you're about to be on bed rest after all the positions I had you in. Number four is definitely in there. How many days do you need to recover Mrs. Saint Baptiste?" The silly grin that was stamped across his face displaying his straight white teeth, only made me laugh at how foolish he was.

"You are such a mess. Bring me my baby and my food."

He sauntered over to me, handed me the tray of food, and sat at the edge of the bed still holding Miracle. Saint was a great father and that's why part of me felt guilty for denying him of something we both wanted. We handled Miracle's birth differently. He saw it as a sign for us to continue our family. I, on the other hand, saw it as an end to the heartbreak of losing any more children.

Now that over a year had passed, I was regretting making that decision alone more and more. Essentially, I regretted it as soon as Miracle turned six months because I did really want another baby. Some women didn't care for motherhood but not me. In my heart, I knew I was made for it. It wasn't my only purpose, but it was one of them. Providing my children with a home filled with love and a nurturing spirit, would always be one of them.

With Saint bringing up the idea of having one more baby, the self-imposed anxiety that had been building up for the past few months was threatening to overflow at any point. It was only a matter of time before he stopped mentioning it jokingly and want to have an in-depth conversation. One that I was not ready to have.

"As usual, I did my thing," Saint said. He watched me eat my ham and spinach omelet as he bounced our daughter on his lap. "Go ahead and say it baby. You were trying to downplay my spaghetti last night. Say something about my cooking now."

Saint Baptiste was a great cook. He even improved my cooking skills. There were a few dishes that I was able to surpass him in but not many. He prepared everything from scratch. For example, the spaghetti he made; the noodles and meat sauce were both made the day before. It was just that he cooked the same three dishes whenever he cooked his two days a week.

"You did your thing babe. All I was saying was that you cook the same three meals every time it's your night to cook."

"That's because those are Heaven's favorites. I have to make sure my first baby girl is happy."

"What about SJ?"

"That little nigga likes you more than he likes me. I'm not worried about his favorites," he said with a scowl on his face.

It was funny because SJ's favorites were the exact same as Heaven's. After gaining my composure from laughing at how hurt he sounded, I said, "Don't call my baby that. He may like me more, but he acts just like you."

"That's fine because I have Heaven and Miracle," Saint responded and shrugged his broad shoulders. Soon after, a strained look appeared on his face.

Placing my fork back on the plate, I said, "Tell me what's on your mind babe."

He let out a soft groan, "There's something I've been wanting to talk to you about babe, all jokes aside."

The inevitable was about to happen and I was going to

have to deal with the aftermath of it all. After sitting my half-eaten tray of food on the nightstand, I took Miracle from him. She may have been more of a daddy's girl than Heaven because she acted like she didn't want to come to me. Heaven never played me like that. Instead of holding her, I sat her on our king size bed to play around.

"Look baby, I want us to grow our family and complete it. Four has always been our number and I still want that. It may come off as selfish, I know that, but it's what I want for us. What I thought we both wanted for us. If anything has changed, tell me because I can sense the hesitation from you. There's a shift in you. I can feel it, but I can't quite understand it. That's never happened in our marriage before."

He was trying his best to handle his emotions, but I could feel it in his aura. My decision to have my tubes tied without his knowledge would break him. Rather than telling him what I did, I chose to tell him how I felt after giving birth to Miracle.

"That is what I wanted for us. A large part of me still wants that baby. It's just that after having two miscarriages and finally being able to carry Miracle full-term, took a lot of my pain away but the happiness didn't replace all the grieving that we both did. At the time, it made more sense to stop so that we didn't have to endure that pain anymore."

"See, I saw it as the miracle to our next *Blessing*."

The way he said blessing threw me off. I knew I would regret asking but I asked anyway, "Are you using blessing as a noun or...?"

A Cheshire grin formed on his face, "Nope. That would be our little girl's name. I dreamt about it the night Miracle was born."

"What if I were to have a boy?"

"God wouldn't do that to me. Our last one would definitely be a girl. We don't need any more mama's boys in the house. Two is enough."

"Two?" I asked.

"Yeah, me and Saint Jr." I couldn't help but to laugh at just how serious he was.

"You're impossible. What time are you going into work today?" I asked, changing the subject. The timing wasn't right to confess to him what I had done. He was already suspicious that I was holding something back.

"I'm not. Ashley has everything under control. Today is going to be family day. I figured we could go to Matheson Hammock Park. It's close by so if the kid's get restless, we can hurry up and bring them back home for a nap."

"We're only going because that's Heaven's favorite park." I shook my head at him. Heaven was a little diva. Saint was an accomplice in making her that way, but she got that attitude from his mom. SJ wasn't as difficult as she was. He went with the flow, just like his dad. He'd eat whatever she ate and did whatever she wanted to do.

"That's baby girl." He winked at me before getting up from the bed. "You get ready and I'll finish getting the kids ready." Miracle reached for him to pick her up. When he left out the room, I got out of bed and prepared for the day. It was always hot in Miami and today was not an exception. I threw on an orange, light material spaghetti strapped sundress with a pair of tan thong sandals.

Saint was waiting for me at the front door with our two girls matching in pink shorts and white t-shirts. SJ matched him, wearing a plain white t-shirt and black basketball shorts. He lived to do the family thing. It was like the day we decided to do start a family, he did a full one eighty. The Saint I met ten years ago was a more reckless version of the man he was today. In his past profession, he had to be that way. He had always made smart decisions, but he lived for the moment, never planning for his future. He only planned for those around him to be prepared to continue life without him. Us having children gave him more than just me to live for. He was now living for himself, so that he could always be a role model for our children.

When we got to the park, Heaven took off towards the atoll pool. SJ followed right behind her. Saint had packed their bathing suits, so they would be able to enjoy the water. As badly as I didn't want Heaven to wet her thick curly hair, trying to stop her was pointless. I would just have to wash it and comb it when we made it back home. It was crazy to think the two of them would be turning four in the matter of weeks. As we both played with the children in the water, I thought back on how he and I first met and how much our life had changed since then. The loved that we shared, the bond that we had created, and the family unit that he desperately wanted to build on, were things I never wanted to lose. I was going to tell him soon but today was too perfect to ruin.

CHAPTER 5

*S*aint

10 years ago-Dice's house party

My right-hand Jonas, his younger brother Mac, and I had just pulled up to Dice's house party. I would've rather been in my hotel room taking a nap or laid up with whichever one my girls were available for the night. This just wasn't my scene. I preferred to lay low. Being at a house party in Inglewood, Nashville wasn't lowkey at all. Especially with me being in town temporarily.

"You good?" Jonas asked me as we sat in the car. He and Mac were my brothers from another mother. Jonas was two years younger than me. We both moved from the islands around the same time. Growing up foreign in a new country wasn't easy. My English wasn't good enough and Jonas didn't speak English at all. What bonded us was the Creole language. I heard him speaking it one day to his little brother, Mac. At first, I thought it was St. Lucian Creole but the further I listened, I was able to tell there was a slight difference. After that day, we just clicked. We ran the streets together from day one. He and I had a lot in common, we did what we had to do to provide a better life for our families, but we wouldn't dare tell them what we really did.

We'd been in the game together for ten years starting, at the age of thirteen and fifteen. He and I worked equally as hard to become the head of our own organization. Our connects, be it they were Columbians, trusted us more than they did others. For the first time since coming to America, being foreigners was beneficial to us. We had more money than we knew what to do with, but you wouldn't be able to tell because we weren't flashy. Our names spoke volumes in the streets, but nobody could put faces to the names other than those close to us. That was one of the most important things our OG taught us. We had made it ten years without any arrests or charges. There wasn't any stopping us.

"This ain't my type of party," I said to Jonas.

"True but sometimes you got to do things outside of the ordinary, man. You never know what you might find."

"There you go thinking you're dropping knowledge, ol' wise ass nigga," I responded.

The three of us started laughing because for Jonas to only be twenty-three, that nigga was wise as hell. Half of the time his wisdom kept us from making illogical decisions. I was smart but sometimes being hot-tempered got the best of me. Jonas' wisdom and my street smarts were the main reasons we were at the top of the game. I had South Florida on lock while he had all of Tennessee on lock. Moving down to Florida when Ace got accepted into FIU, was the best decision I made for our organization. I was able to get closer to our connect and get better product at a better price. The product that Jonas was slinging in Tennessee was one of a kind.

"Whatever nigga. You'll thank me later. Stop acting like you didn't need this break."

Ignoring him, I looked back at the rearview mirror to see his little brother smiling hard as hell. "Mac, why is your young ass even out here?"

Mac was like a little brother to me, thus I treated him no differently than I treated Ace. Both Jonas and I made sure to keep him out of our dealings but deep down, I could tell he wanted to be a part of it. Jonas kept him close enough to make sure he didn't go astray. The last thing we wanted was for someone to put him in a position that would mess up his future. The closer we kept him to us, the further he would be from someone pulling him into the game. Mac handled all our numbers to make sure everything appeared legit with the few legal businesses that we owned. That was the closest he was going to get into the organization.

The little nigga was a genius in technology, math, and science. He was only little in age because he was built like a linebacker with pure muscle. He played football and was number one in his class. He had just turned seventeen and was about to graduate high school.

"I wanted to hang with my two older brothers before I moved," he answered.

Mac had gotten a full ride to University of Tennessee to play football and an academic scholarship to Massachusetts Institution of Technology. Jonas wanted him to take the MIT scholarship but last I heard, he hadn't made up his mind. Even though he would've been going to UT for football, from what I knew, their academic programs were good.

"Enough of the talking. Are we going in or not?" Jonas asked.

"Who you got waiting in there that got you rushing us?" I asked, causing Mac to start laughing again.

"Are we going in or not, nigga?"

"Yeah we are. Calm your ass down. Vibe isn't off, so I'm cool with it," I answered. We got out of Jonas' all black Dodge Camaro and headed towards the house. That's what I meant when I said we weren't flashy. He was able to afford a brand-new Benz, but homie bought a Camaro.

Dice's house was in the middle of the hood. Jonas and I met him three years ago right when we started our organization. He was one of the most solid men on our team. He did a bid two weeks after he joined our organization. That helped him prove his loyalty to us. Dice's name had two meanings; he was a beast at shooting dice and if someone crossed him, well you can figure the rest out.

Dice was on the porch surrounded by a few people I recognized but mostly people I didn't. I was certain that none recognized me.

"Look who decided to pull up on us," he greeted me before pulling me in for a brotherly hug. He did the same to Jonas and Mac.

"Yeah, had to come through." I planned to see him, but it wasn't at this house party. This was only my second day in Nashville.

"Well y'all enjoy y'all selves. There's liquor, food, and women."

The women didn't interest me. I had enough that I was already dealing with. Being young had my views on monogamy messed up. I didn't necessarily like the idea of cheating on a woman. What I would do is have situation-ships. We had the benefit of doing everything that was done in a relationship but without the title, therefore I didn't feel guilty about having multiple women. It was wrong but I made sure they were all aware that they weren't the only one I was involved with. The decision was up to them if they wanted to stay or not. Now if I was ever to date a woman exclusively, my focus would solely be on her, but I didn't have the desire to be monogamous.

Marriage and family were never the objective, even though my parents provided me with a great example of what that was. I just preferred the "we were for the moment". However long that moment lasted was fine with me. Whether it was a month or two years, it didn't matter because marriage and having a family wasn't meant for everybody. Being in the profession that I was in didn't offer me the privilege to have all of that. Deep down, I wanted what my parents had—the love and building a strong family unit as husband and wife. It just didn't seem possible. So, for the time being, I was dealing with situationships.

Once we were inside, I pulled out my Henny-filled flask. I might've agreed to be at the house party, but I wasn't drinking or eating from anybody. The atmosphere was cool though. What caught my attention almost knocked the air out of my lungs. My feet started moving before I could even realize what was happening. I almost tripped over myself trying to get to her. The moment our eyes connected, her spirit told me she needed me just as much as I needed her.

She was beautiful. Her auburn colored, curly hair was in an afro with a side part. Her smooth pecan colored skin was begging me to touch it. She was extremely curvy. Her wide hips were mesmerizing. Her breasts were big but not outrageous. It wasn't until the person next to her cleared her throat, did I notice there was someone else there. It was a young woman that favored her. I assumed that they were family. I bent down and whispered in Miss Pecan's ear, to meet me on the porch and left out of the party. By that time the party was in full affect, leaving the porch empty. I was out there for approximately ten minutes before she crept out the front door. There had to be something about her to make me wait ten whole minutes. Being impatient was one of the things that I was known for.

The light from the moon peered on us and I was able to see her face better. She was drop dead gorgeous. She was wearing high waisted jeans and a loose-fitting crop top. Her attire was my indication that she didn't attend house parties often. All of the women there were either in short skirts or shorts and halter tops.

"You wanted to talk to me?" she asked timidly. She was doing her best not to make eye contact and that bothered me.

"Can you do me a favor?"

"It depends on what it is," she answered while still refusing to make eye contact.

"Look at me in my eyes when we're talking."

"Why?"

I let out a soft chuckle and shifted my weight to the banister that was behind me. Leaning on it, I folded my arms across my chest, "One, it's rude not to. Two, it makes me feel like I can't trust you when you don't."

"What makes you think I want you to trust me?"

I ignored her question and said, "Your eyes are the gateway to your soul."

"What makes you think I want you to see inside my soul?"

This time I chose to answer her question. "You've already given me a glimpse and now I want all the way in."

We spent the rest of the night on the porch talking about what we wanted out of life, what love meant to us, and our futures. She didn't judge me for my point of views on planning for my future and love. She did, however, have me thinking it was possible for them to change.

"From what you've told me, you come from a good family. Why would you not want that for yourself?" she asked.

"Honestly, I do want it. It's just with the way my life is at the moment, it's better not to think about."

"The future isn't important to you?" This time she stared straight into me. It almost as if she was staring past me, waiting for me to respond.

"I live for the present," I replied before grabbing her hand to hold inside mine.

"The future is all I have," she said before removing her hand. Shortly after, the person she was with, came out to inform her it was time for them to leave. I offered to take them home since neither drove there, but Miss Pecan declined. I didn't drive either, but it would've been nothing to borrow Jonas' car. We made sure to exchange contact information after I got her to agree to have breakfast with me in the morning. When they disappeared in the direction they were headed, I realized I hadn't gotten her name. I saved her number under Miss Pecan after which I proceeded to delete and block every other woman that was in my phone.

The rest of my night was spent on the porch texting her. It was around three in the morning when Mac and Jonas emerged from the house party. By that time, everything was starting to die down. Mac didn't drink, so he volunteered to drive. I was cool with it because I wanted to continue texting Miss Pecan. When I made it to my hotel room, she hadn't replied to my text to inform me of the time and place for breakfast. I finally ended up closing my eyes at four AM, hoping that I would wake up to a text from her.

CHAPTER 6

Saint

10 years ago-morning after Dice's house party

My first instinct every morning was to check the time. This morning was different. I was checking to see if she had texted me back from earlier. My heart sunk when I saw that she had read my message but hadn't replied. With the way our energies matched one another, it didn't make sense for her not to text back. Rather than dwell on it, I got up to prepare for the day. Someone at the house party had to know who she was so if she didn't reply, I was just going to have Dice ask around. Even though I didn't know her real name, all I had to do was describe what she was wearing.

After getting out the shower, I grabbed my phone from the bed. Still no text from Miss Pecan. Just when I was about to call Dice and see what type of information I could get from him, my phone vibrated in my hand. It was her confirming the time and place. Looking at the time, I saw that I had forty-five minutes to be at the breakfast spot. She was the one that picked it out and I had no idea where it was. It hadn't been that long since I left Nashville, but I'd never heard of Arizona's Diner.

Typing the address in my GPS, I saw that it wasn't too far from my hotel. I threw on a pair of black basketball shorts, black Nikes, and a matching black t-shirt. Afterwards, I left out the room to run a quick errand before meeting with her at the diner.

Once I was done with my errand, I rushed over to Arizona's Diner that was off of Charlotte Pike. The diner was small but hopefully the food was good. I made it right at ten o'clock, the time we had agreed on. She didn't show up until fifteen minutes after ten. I stood up and pulled her into a hug before she sat across from me in our booth. Seeing her in the daytime gave me the opportunity to appreciate her natural beauty. Her skin glistened. Her eyes easily put me in a mindless trance. Her body...

The waitress immediately came over and took our orders. She ordered a ham and spinach omelet with a side of pancakes and I had toast with a side of eggs and sausage. They weren't about to ruin pancakes for me. The only pancakes I ate were my Ma's, Jolie Baptiste. The place wasn't too busy therefore we got our food relatively fast. Even if the food turned out to be mediocre at least the service was good.

I watched her take a few bites of her food before deciding to break the silence, "Are you going to make a habit of keeping me waiting?"

She didn't look up from her food while asking, "What are you talking about?"

I shook my head, "Ten minutes last night, your message this morning, and fifteen minutes for breakfast. I'm not saying that I have a problem waiting for you. What I'm saying is that I want to know if you're going to make it a habit of it. That way I can adjust to waiting on you for the rest of my life."

She finally looked up at me and allowed me to really stare into her eyes for the first time. Hints of mystery and pain were concealed behind them. But most importantly, I saw the longing for love and peace.

"I'm not naïve," she said.

"Never said you were."

"Then don't say shit like that to me," she growled at me. Most men might've been offended but I wasn't most men. She had a reason to feel the way she did. One that I wasn't aware of but nevertheless, was there.

"You don't like to hear the truth?" I asked, sliding further down into my seat.

"Who's to say your words are true?"

"Nobody but me. I've never been a liar though. There's no point in me starting now."

"I've heard that before."

"Was it from me?" She slowly shook her head, and I continued before she could, "Then that doesn't apply to me. I'm not understanding this energy you're coming with. We connected well last night. You even agreed to have breakfast with me."

"How many women do you know that would turn down a free meal?" She smiled so big, I couldn't help but to laugh.

According to her, there weren't many women that would turn it down. That helped lightening up the mood some. Miss Pecan opened up eventually and everything started flowing like it did the night before. She told me Arizona's Diner was her favorite breakfast spot because they served the best blueberry pancakes. Not many people knew about the place and that's why she liked it. She loved going there to get away. She was ok with sharing something sacred like that with me, so maybe this hard exterior she was showing me was all a front. It was a small diner, but it was her haven from whatever life was throwing at her. More time with her would be the only thing that would give the information as to what it was. She was guarded but that wasn't going deter me from her. I had confidence in what we both felt.

"How are old are you?" she asked me.

"Twenty-five. You?"

Instead of answering, she removed her ID from her purse. She held it up to show me her picture and birthday, triggering me to immediately start sweating. "You're only eighteen. Damn." I rubbed my hand down my freshly cut fade.

She was legal but she was young as hell. Way younger than any woman that I ever dealt with. One part of me wanted to tell her bye and keep it moving. The other part of me—the important part, told me to stay. It convinced me get to know her more and make my decision to pursue her, based on that. It told me that it was a sign that she was legal and that she was forthcoming about it.

"Cool. That's cool. Yeah, we're cool. Cool. That's cool. Yeah, we're good. Ok. Cool," I said.

She giggled and licked her bottom lip before she asked, "Are you sure?"

"Yeah, we're..."

"Cool," she said before I could finish my sentence, "You said it like five times, trying to convince yourself."

"My bad. I just wasn't expecting you to be eighteen. I'm sure though. Even if it's a friendship, I want you in my life long-term."

"As long as you're cool, I'm cool. Cool. We're cool."

That made us both laugh. I had yet to meet a woman that could match my sense of humor apart from her.

I leaned towards the table and placed my clasped hands on top of it directly in front of me. "Let me ask you a couple of questions and I need honesty because that's what I'm offering to you."

She nodded her head yes and I continued, "How did you and your friend get home? How did you get here? Why did you suddenly stop texting me last night, and why did it take you so long to message me back after having read my message?"

"A couple is two. You asked more than a couple."

"Answer the questions smart ass," I said, prompting her to laugh.

"We walked home because we didn't live far, and I caught the bus here. The phone is my cousin Harmony's phone. I use her phone because I don't own one. She was the one that was with me last night."

I pretty much had figured all that out. I had someone follow them home to guarantee they made it home safely. I saw her getting off the bus as well and she had to ask Harmony for the phone when I had her save my number in. Letting her know I would be right back, I ran out to my car, retrieved what I went out there for, and hurried back inside.

After getting back in my side of the booth, I removed the brand-new iPhone 3GS box from the bag. She refused it at first but after thirty minutes of convincing her that it was just for us to be in contact with each other, she agreed. Then it took another twenty minutes of convincing to let me cover the phone bill since I added her to my account. Then ten more minutes of convincing her to let me take her home. Miss Pecan wasn't going to make this easy for me but she damn sure was proving she was worth it.

When we made it to the apartment that she shared with Harmony, she agreed to have dinner with me as our second date. That didn't take any persuading, but I was prepared for it just in case. It was easy for her to open up to me about her dreams and her aspirations. She even opened up about who she was as a person, but I didn't know anything about her. I didn't know her favorite color, what she did for a living, favorite food—none of the things people learned on a first date. Shit, I still didn't know her name. All of that basic information seemed irrelevant when my goal was to reach her soul.

CHAPTER 7

*A*ngel

10 years ago-night of second date

"How do I look?" I asked my cousin Harmony. We were in her bedroom as I modeled the off-the-shoulder, black peplum dress that I was wearing with matching sandal heels.

I had moved in with her, in her one-bedroom apartment eight months prior. It wasn't much but I was beyond grateful she let me sleep on her couch. We used to live in Boston before she moved to Tennessee. As soon as I was able to afford the chance to leave Boston, I took the few clothes I could and left. All I had was one pair of sneakers, a couple of blouses, and two pairs of jeans when I first moved. I also didn't have a dollar to my name. Now I had a few more clothes but I spent the little money I made, wisely.

Getting a job wasn't an option, consequently, I was broke whenever I first moved to Nashville. My only source of income was braiding hair. That was a problem at first because I didn't know anybody in Nashville, which made it hard to market myself. Thankfully with Harmony working part-time at a clothing store while being a fulltime student, I would braid her hair for free and she would refer clients to me. It had been about six months since I started braiding hair out of her house. It only brought in about two hundred a week, but it was enough to cover all utilities and groceries. That's all Harmony required me to cover. She suggested getting a two-bedroom apartment a month ago, however it wasn't plausible with me having an unstable source of income. Even though I was averaging two hundred a week, there were a week or two that I would only make fifty dollars because I only had one customer booked.

"You look good. I wish we were the same size. That way you wouldn't have to spend money on new clothes for the date."

"I know right. Put some meat on your bones by the next date."

"Soooo, you're saying there will be a next date?"

Looking over myself in the mirror I replied, "Do you think this is a bad idea?"

"Hell no!" she exclaimed. "Angel, the way he was looking at you made me want to get ordained and marry you two off last night."

"Stop. It is not that serious. Mr. Chocolate is twenty-five," I said after seating on the bed next to her. I didn't know his name and I had no plans of asking. I was enjoying the mystery. Not only that, if I asked for his, he would ask for mine in return. I didn't want him to know my name.

"What's your point? Last time I checked, you only had to be eighteen for it to be legal. Why aren't you opened up to the idea of love?"

"Because I'm smart enough to know everything that glitter isn't gold. That's why I'm sleeping on your couch with sixty-five dollars to my name."

"Angel, where you are at now is not your fault. You are better off here than in Boston and we both know that. All the bills are paid, and we've done groceries for the week. Plus, we're going to the mall tomorrow to get you some new clients. You are a dope braider and you're Speedy Gonzales with your hands. That, along with you charging only fifty per head, soon you'll be making more than you make now."

We shared a laugh before I said, "Thank you, cousin. For everything."

"We're all we got. I'll always have your back."

Harmony was the only family that I had. Neither of us knew where our parents were because we were brought to Boston at the age of four after being adopted. Well, we had an idea of where they were but not who they were. It's crazy how you're only able to remember bits and pieces of your life at an early age. I remember our parents being promised that we would have a better life in Boston. There was no better life. There was just pure hell. Harmony was able to leave before I was. However, the moment I saw my chance, I ran.

The second Harmony finished doing my makeup, there was a knock on the door. If that was him, that would be his first strike. He was supposed to text me when he was outside, not come to the door. Our apartment was small with little furniture. I didn't want him judging us without knowing our background. A background that I wasn't open to sharing with anyone. I didn't even want to share my name with him. When I showed him my ID at the restaurant, I made it a point to cover up my name and address. The only thing he was able to see were my picture and birthday. He didn't know mine and I didn't know his. Now I regretted letting him drop me off this morning.

Looking out the peephole, I saw him outside in all his

dark chocolate glory. Being with him wasn't an option but I was definitely going to appreciate his good looks. Opening the door, I stepped outside, quickly shutting the door behind me. He was wearing dark gray sweatpants, a plain white t-shirt, and matching Nikes. Now, I was pissed. Why would he ask me to dress up if he was going to come out in sweats? My money could've still been in my purse, hadn't he specifically requested that I dress up.

"Damn, you look good," he said as his dark brown eyes traced the full length of my body.

"And you're not dressed," I quipped.

"Yeah, there's something I want to talk to you about."

If he wanted to cancel the date, all he had to do was send a text. *The phone.* He was here to pick up the phone. "The phone is inside. Give me a second to grab it for you. I'll be right back."

As I turned around to go inside, he caught me by my right wrist. "What? I didn't come over here for that."

I was certain he came for the phone. It wouldn't be the first time a man gave me something and turned around to take it right back. "Then, why are you here? It can't be for our date because you're not dressed up like you were so damn adamant about."

His eyes soften as he released my hand. "You have trust issues and you're guarded as hell." I stared at him as he continued, "You're constantly making assumptions. All of which are wrong by the way."

"Are they?" I asked. He could say all that he wanted to say, but I was not easily persuaded. Too many people had proven their words couldn't be trusted.

"Hell, yeah they're wrong. Your ass is too young to be as guarded as you are."

"Now look who's the one making assumptions," I stated

as I leaned against the front door, with my arms folded across my chest.

"Valid point. My bad. Just hear me out before you jump to conclusions. Can you do that, please?"

I nodded my head, signaling him to continue. "I have to go back to Miami tonight to tend to my business. The reason I came over instead of texting or calling you is because I want you to come to Miami with me. Before you say no, it'll be just for the night. You'll leave in the morning if that's what you want. I'm a man of word which means, we are going to have our date tonight."

I knew he couldn't have been seriously asking me to go to Miami with him for a night, just so he could keep his word. That didn't make any sense. "Are you for real?" I asked. His serious facial expression said he was, but logic said otherwise.

"Wouldn't be here if I wasn't. Is that a yes?"

"No."

A look of disappointment appeared on his delicious chocolate face. I hated that I was the cause of it. There were several reasons why I couldn't go to Miami with him. Other than the obvious of me only having a few dollars to my name, he and I had only known of each other for a day. We may have shared some of our inner most thoughts and aspirations, but we didn't know each other. It was easy for me to tell him what I wanted, my thoughts, and anything that didn't have to do with my past or present. My future was my hope, and no one could judge me for it. My past didn't break me, but it made me cautious of people's true intentions.

"Why not? Give me five good reasons as to why you won't go?"

My voice heightened as I asked, "Five?"

Why couldn't this man just take no for an answer? A rational person would've asked for one. But here this man was asking for not one, not two, but five different reasons. All of the good ones I had, I wasn't comfortable sharing with him.

"Yep, five. I'll determine if they are good or not," he said as a wide grin tugged at his full lips. I had well over five that I wasn't willing to share. We stared at each other for almost a minute before he spoke up again.

"I really want this. Bad." Him making that declaration, led me to licking my bottom lip. "What do I have to do to get you to agree to come to Miami with me?"

"There's nothing you can do." Most woman would've jumped at him offering a trip to Miami. Thing was, I wasn't most women and most women sure as hell hadn't been through what I went through. Whatever he wanted in return wasn't anything I had to offer.

"Where's your cousin?"

"She's inside. Why?"

"Have her come out here real quick. I have to ask her something."

Against my better judgement, I went back inside closing the door behind me. There was no way I was going to invite him in. Harmony was all too happy to come out and talk to him after I gave her a quick rundown of what happened. We both stepped back outside to find Mr. Chocolate leaning against the rail waiting for us. He shook Harmony's hand before he started talking. She had the most ridiculous smile on her face and I just wanted to slap it off. I already knew whatever it was he planned on talking to her about, she was going to go along with it.

She and I grew up the same, but she had more of a trusting nature. Maybe I would've been the same way hadn't I gone through my last experience with my ex. Harmony and I both believed in watching for patterns and consistency. We were both pretty good at reading people and feeling people's vibes. My ex messed my head up so bad that I didn't trust that ability anymore. Saint's vibe told me it was ok to give him a chance, which was why I opened up to him some. I just couldn't let myself be in that same predicament, yet again.

"It's nice to see you again, cousin," he said, causing Harmony to blush. "I'm trying to keep my word by taking your cousin on a date tonight. Do either one of you have anything planned for the next three days?"

"No, we don't." My mouth fell open as I listened to Harmony lie. I had two hair appointments scheduled in two days. She also had to a midday shift tomorrow at the clothing store.

"Good. If you could pack you and her a bag to take to Miami, that would be great. Here is my credit card." He went into his pocket, pulled out his wallet, and handed her his card.

"Use it to book the plane tickets and a room at the hotel of her choice. When you've done that, give her the card. She's stubborn but I can tell you're not. Can you do those things for me?"

Just like I knew she would, she agreed to all of his requests. Without saying another word, he planted a kiss on my forehead, gave Harmony a hug, and left. As soon as we made it inside, Harmony went straight to her room to start packing. I sat at the edge of the bed, watching her go through her closet.

"We're not going to Miami with him, Harmony."

"Who's not going? This credit card that he freely handed us, says otherwise."

"I'm serious about this. What does he get out of this?"

"You," she stated. "Sometimes that's all a man wants. You."

"Mr. Chocolate..." Before I could finish, she cut me off.

"Saint."

"Huh?"

"His name is Saint. It's on his card. Wait until he finds out your name is Angel. You two are about to be a match made in heaven."

"He's not going to. We're not using that card," I said.

Harmony turned around and brought her hands to her semi-wide hips. "The hell we're not! You heard that man. He gave us clear instructions and I plan to follow them." She continued, "I get it Angel, I really do. You have to stop doing what you're doing. You see the good in him but because of your ex, you're blocking yourself from it."

"I thought my ex had good in him, too."

"No you didn't. We both smelled that he wasn't shit from a mile away. Your circumstances were why we chose to ignore it."

She was absolutely right. I knew my ex was the devil reincarnated. He was manipulative and vindictive, even though that's not how he presented himself at first. I was in a bad situation before him and I needed a way out. He was my way out. I just didn't think it would've been worse than the hell that I was living in at the time. It didn't cross my mind that my freedom from one hell would've led to bondage to another one. He viewed himself as my liberator; he wasn't that in the least.

The day he and I first met, he was amiable. He knew my situation and offered me an out, in exchange I'd be his girl-friend. Call me young and dumb but I fell for it. I thought we could learn to love each other, not realizing the only way love could be sustained was the one that came naturally. Some things weren't meant to be forced and love was definitely one of them. At first, it was good. I was finally in an environment that didn't bring physical, emotional, or mental pain. It quickly changed after two weeks of living in the fake paradise that he retained me in.

One day he came home and punched me in stomach because someone stole from him. His workers saw his weakness, in turn he exercised his strength on me. It only got worst from there. I could take the beatings, the verbal abuse, and the mental destruction. My upbringing made me numbed to it. It granted me the luxury of escaping during the moments of abuse.

After a few months of having to deal with it, I found my escape. He had left some money on the dresser before leaving to hang out with his brother. I waited close to thirty minutes to make sure he wasn't coming back. I sent him a text, telling him that I was going to the grocery store to buy me enough time before he started looking for me. Only having grabbed a couple of outfits and three hundred dollars from the nightstand, I left his house that day, heading straight to the bus station to buy a one-way ticket to Nashville. I was certain he wouldn't miss a few missing outfits. Having already given him the excuse that I was going to the grocery store, he wouldn't have thought much about the missing money either. I made sure to leave my cell phone at home so that he wouldn't be able to track me. In his mind I was indebted to him with my life. That wasn't the type of relationship I'd wish on my worst enemy.

"All I'm saying is, don't write Saint off because of an asshole that wasn't shit to begin with." She shrugged her shoulders and turned back around to retrieve more clothes from the closet.

Saint did open up himself, I could read him. No matter how hard I fought it, he saw me. The real me. It wasn't something I was even trying to comprehend because I didn't need him involved in my mess. He already proved himself to be the type of man to find a solution to anything that posed a threat to something he wanted. That was how I ended up with a brand-new phone that I initially declined. That was the exact same reason Harmony was on her phone booking our plane tickets to Miami. As much as I wanted to believe in the good that I saw in Saint, I had to protect him from the evil of my past.

CHAPTER 8

*S*aint

10 years ago- Miami: later that same night

My flight got in an hour before theirs was scheduled to. They had to catch a different flight since mine was fully booked. The call from Loco, my second-in-command, couldn't have come in at a worse time but until Miss Pecan showed me that I was what she wanted, the streets came first. It always came first and up until we talked at Dice's party, I thought it always would. The type of nigga I was, didn't believe in love at first sight. However, the connection I felt when I gravitated towards her was hands down the closest thing to it. I'd be a damn fool not to chase that shit and, Jolie Baptiste didn't raise any fools.

"How do you know this girl ain't after your money?" Loco asked.

He was a Dominican Afro-Latino that I had met through my connect. Unlike me, he was born in America. He worked his way up and earned his spot. I didn't believe in handing shit out to anybody. I didn't trust him like I trusted Jonas or Dice, but I needed someone that knew

Miami. I trusted Dice when it came to the streets and him protecting our organization. I didn't trust Loco with my life, but I trusted him with his. Which meant he wouldn't do anything stupid to cross me if he viewed his life as something of value. Other than Ace and Jonas, my trust in people wasn't solid when it came to my personal life.

"Don't refer to her as this girl, nigga." That shit rubbed me the wrong way. Granted she was young, but Miss Pecan was a grown ass woman. I didn't even bother to answer Loco's question. The only person I answered to, was my Ma. That nigga was not her, therefore his question didn't warrant a response.

I didn't care what any man said. When a woman was after money or status, you saw it. You could literally feel it. Some women were devious, but they would always give you signs at first contact. Whether you choose to ignore it, that was solely up to you. In my line of work, I paid attention to all signs. So far, Miss Pecan hadn't given me any. She wasn't playing hard to get. She was fighting herself. She was torn between what she wanted and what she went through. I could tell from our first conversation.

Instead of going home when Loco came to drop my car off to me at the airport, I decided to wait for Harmony and Miss Pecan to arrive. That way, I could drop them off at their hotel, instead of sending a driver. Loco was supposed to simply drop my car off and find a way home. Him still being there was starting to irritate me.

"Why are you still here, Loco?"

"You said she was coming down with her cousin. I'm trying to see what her cousin is about."

He must've lost his damn mind from the time I left Miami and had just returned. "Nah, you're blind nigga."

"What?" he asked with a confused expression. His hair

was cut low and he had a grill in his mouth. Loco had three diamond chains draped around his thick neck. A diamond ring on each finger. A whole lot of unnecessary shit. Shit like that was asking for unwanted attention from the wrong people. Other than anything business-related, I wouldn't be caught dead with that nigga.

"You are blind when it comes to her cousin, so ain't nothing for you to see. I'll hit you up later on tonight." There was no way in hell I was going to let Loco anywhere near Harmony. Everyone had a role in life and when you started switching their roles, that's when you messed yourself up. Loco was cool for business but not personal. The minute I gave him any inclination that he had room to be anything outside of my second-in-command, he would run with it. That shit was never going to happen.

"Damn, it's like that?"

"Yeah. You know you, or do I need to remind you of who you are?"

He waved his hands up in surrender and walked away without saying another word. He knew he didn't have anything to offer but false hope and broken promises. I may have not put into much thought into my future with a woman but that didn't take away from me knowing just how valuable they were. How could I not? My mom was my leading example of everything a good woman should embody. She made sure both my brother and I knew how to treat women. I was never going to be the man that put a woman in a position to set her up for a broken heart. That's partially why I had stopped doing the long-term situationships.

As soon as Loco left, I was able to sit down and gather my thoughts. It didn't make sense that I didn't know any of her basic information but yet, here I was at Miami

International Airport, waiting for her and her cousin to arrive. That's how badly I wanted to take her on this second date. None of that mattered as long as I was able to keep my word. It was worth seeing if I should have faith in what I was feeling. Every part of me had a hunger to see where faith would lead us to.

A man like me didn't believe in coincidences. Everything happened for a reason, whether we were aware of it or not. I didn't have any negative thoughts about Dice's house party because I was destined to meet her there at that time, and in that moment. Fate brought us together. It was now up to me to find the reason as to why.

With my head down, I felt her before I saw her. "Saint." Her angelic voice touched my ears sending shivers down my spine.

I lifted my head to find Miss Pecan standing in front of me, wearing a tight-fitting purple maxi dress. Each curve of her body was accentuated, triggering my body to react in an unfamiliar way. Heart racing, palm sweating, speechless. As I stared into her eyes, an epiphany hit me almost taking all of the oxygen out of my lungs.

She was the one.

Even with me not knowing her name, in my heart I knew she was the one. Even without me knowing her past, the promise and hope in her eyes were my guarantee of our future. Standing up from my seat, I grabbed her by her waist and pulled her into me for a hug. Her body pushed into mine and I felt us becoming one. The woman that I left in Nashville a few hours ago, wasn't the same one that was tightly enclosed in my arms. Her spirit felt opened.

"Now that you know my name, can I finally know yours?" I whispered in her ear.

It was easy for me to notice that she was being secretive

about certain aspects of her life. Just like I had noticed that she didn't have a phone, I peeped how she covered up her name on her ID when she showed it to me at Arizona's Diner. I also noticed that it was a basic ID. Not a license but a regular Tennessee identification card. Being observant was what kept me in the streets and out of jail. It was a way of life for me. The need to have her in my life was strong, so I needed whatever we were going to be with each other, to be natural. Therefore, being attentive was a must with her.

"Angel."

Without control, I let out a soft chuckle and pulled away. I scratched the top of my head before laughing again. "You for real?"

"Yes, my name is Angel."

"A match made in heaven," Harmony said. I quickly gave her a hug before drawing Angel back into my arms. Once again, I hadn't noticed that she was next to Angel. That's just how much Angel captivated me. Merely the thought of her erased any other woman from my mind and eyesight. Harmony was very attractive. She and Angel favored but she was a shade darker. She was smaller than Angel in size and stature, as well but you could easily tell two were related. I would've picked them as sisters and not cousins.

"My bad, Harmony."

"It's cool. You're all caught up in my cousin. I can't even complain because it got me a mini vacation to Miami," she said before doing a quick dance.

Angel and I laughed at how silly she was being. I didn't mind giving her a mini vacation. She gave me what I wanted in return. Harmony's aura was different than Angel's. She wasn't as guarded and a bit more trusting. She wasn't naïve by a long shot but definitely had more of a trusting nature than Angel.

"Let me know whenever you're ready for that full vacation, I got you." I honestly would've given her anything to sway Angel to come to Miami. This second date was important to me. I had to show her that I was a man of my word. There was no way that she would've taken my pursuit seriously if I would've cancelled.

They each only brought a backpack, which meant they only intended on spending the three days. Initially, that's what I offered because I figured that Angel would say no to anything more than that. After dinner tonight, I was going to see if I could turn three days into two weeks. If she was willing to give me more, I'd take it. If Harmony had to be there, then I was going to make sure that happened.

We were finally on the way to their hotel at nine o'clock. The plan was to drop them off and have a driver return to pick up Angel and bring her to where our second date would be. I had someone setting it up for me, but I had to make sure it was to my liking.

Having to come back to Miami to handle, things messed up my plans with Angel. The date that I had originally planned had to be cancelled. Luckily, I was quick on my feet, so I was able to come up with something almost as good. The original plan was to rent out a kitchen, cook for her, and share a private dinner together. Other than my Ma, no other woman could claim that they tasted my food before. I had spent the whole day preparing for it but unfortunately, that would have to wait. Since I had to cancel it, I thought the best way to persuade her into coming to Miami was to do it in person, which is exactly what I did.

Looking over at her in the passenger seat of my car, I

knew I made the right choice. "How much time do you think you need to get ready?"

"For what?" A look of misunderstanding spread across her beautifully sculpted face. She must've assumed that our date was going to rescheduled for the next day, but it was happening tonight.

"Our second date. I want us to have it tonight."

"I thought you would want to do it tomorrow or another day."

"What did we say about making assumptions?" I asked her.

She rolled her eyes at me before shaking her head. Just like I thought, she expected me to not keep my word. In a way, it bothered me because I'd never had someone doubt me before. Not my family, not anyone in my organization, and definitely not the streets. That doubt that she was exhibiting was my guide to breaking down the wall that shielded her heart. I'd have to get her to believe in me with more than my words. My actions had to support every word that I would speak into her. Words weren't going to be enough to make her heart my permanent home. Tonight, I was going to start knocking down that wall down completely. Patience was never my strong suit. If I wanted something, I did everything within my power to get it as quickly as possible. Angel's spirit, heart, body, all of her would be mine when the time was right. I just had to show her that I was deserving of it all, in order for her to let it happen naturally.

After dropping Harmony and Angel off at their hotel, I rushed to Miami Beach. That's where I had Jonas' cousin, Pierre, setting up the second date for me. He wanted to be a chef and if I were to ever get out the game, I would make sure that happened. I was able to get him to cook us a nice meal. When I made it there, everything was almost set up. I sent Angel a quick text, letting her know that I was sending a car to pick her up.

More than anything, I wanted tonight to be intimate. There were things that I had to share with her, so that we could build something together. Meeting Angel gave me a possibility of a life that didn't involve me living like there was no tomorrow. It gave me a future to look forward to. No amount of money could do that for me. The streets would never be able to do that for me. The possibility of a life with her by my side, did that for me.

𝒶 ngel

10 years ago- Miami: second date

As I sat in the car that Saint sent to take me to the location of our second date, I reflected on the conversation Harmony and I had on the way to the airport. I had no idea what he did or who he was outside of our connection, but he clearly was someone of importance to have been able to send a car.

"Listen to your intuition," Harmony stated. *We were seated in the back of the car that Saint had come pick us up to take us to the airport.*

"What do you mean?" I knew what she meant but I knew more than anything, I needed her to say it.

"Listen to your intuition. What is it telling you? No filter."

I chewed on the inside of my right cheek as I closed my eyes. I shut down the idea of logic because logic told me I was crazy to be on my way to Miami to have a second date with a man, I didn't know if he even met my standards. My heart opened up. She told me that she knew him. She told me

to give her a chance to explore what he was going to offer her.
My spirit calmed down the torment of my past and reminded
me that the few times that I had been in his presence, she was
at peace. My spirit had never known peace until him.

"What is it telling you?" Harmony asked again.

"Open up to him and give him a real chance," I said
before a one-sided smile tugged at the corner of my lip. Saint
wasn't my ex-boyfriend or like anyone in my past. All I had
to do was give him a genuine chance to prove that to me. It
was obvious I would regret it if I didn't.

Once the car halted, I realized that we were at the
beach. The driver stepped out of the car to open my door,
but Saint stopped him. I watched through the window as
the two had a whispered exchange before Saint opened the
door for me. He reached for me with his hand and I took
that moment to admire his melanin rich skin nicely draped
in his beige dress shirt and navy-blue slacks. To say he
cleaned up nice was a definite understatement. Saint looked
damn good and by the smile that graced his manly-carved
face, he was very well aware of that. He smelled even better
as I took a moment to rejoice internally, from having the
pleasure of his cologne mixed with his natural scent assault
my airway.

We took off our shoes and he led me to a table in the
middle of the sand that was adorned with white rose petals,
candles, plates, and two wine glasses. Next to it was a
smaller table with a bottle of Hennessey, sparkling grape
juice, and three covered plates. He pulled out my chair
before walking around and taking his place across from me.

"What do you think?" he asked the second he sat down.

"You are something else, you know that?" I asked while
shaking my head at him. Saint could've easily canceled our
date. He could've gone back to Miami and he and I would

have never seen each other again. As an alternative, he chose to come to the apartment I shared with my cousin, to ask me to come to Miami for our date.

He rubbed his hand over his beard and bit his bottom lip. "Is that a good or bad thing?"

"Only you can answer that question," I responded. Giving Saint a chance meant that I was not only opening myself to possibility of love but hurt. That scared me more than anything that I endured in the past. I didn't know how much more pain I was able to take before becoming bitter. That's something I fought through daily growing up. Saint couldn't be the catalyst that catapulted me into a life of acrimony.

Instead of answering, he nodded his head and stood up. He grabbed the wine glasses from the table. What he did next, caused me to burst out into a loud laughter. I watched Saint pour Hennessy and sparkling grape juice into the two wine glasses. When he made it back to the table, he handed me the wine glass of sparkling grape juice before returning to his place across from me.

"Are you serious?"

"What?" he asked with genuine confusion saturating his deep, sultry voice.

"You're drinking Hennessey out of a wine glass and you gave me sparkling grape juice."

He shrugged his broad muscular shoulders before saying, "Hennessy is the only liquor I drink. I don't drink wine and you aren't twenty-one yet. The glasses are more so for ambiance."

I nodded my head and resumed what he was saying, "Listen baby, there's no point in putting on a show, I am who I am. I'm a little unpolished but I wanted to show you that I will cater to you the best way I know how. You'll get fancy shit but it's going to be sincerely to show you my intentions. I want you more than I've ever wanted anyone. I want to figure out what this is, more than anything."

Once he was finished talking, he gulped down his Hennessey as he waited for my reply. He did put a lot into tonight. Not for one second was it overlooked. A candlelight dinner on the beach was not what I imagined when he asked me to join him for a second date. We sat there in silence, purely staring at each other. His eyes never strayed from mine.

Deciding to finally break the silence I said, "My trust is broken. I'm a flawed person. There are insecurities that I battle with daily. I'm nowhere near perfect Saint."

I wasn't ready to offer him the details of my past, but it was only right that I made him aware of what he was asking for. If he wanted my heart, he had to know that he was going to get one that was tampered with. One that was damaged. One that never learned how to give or receive love.

"I never asked for perfection babe. What I'm asking is a chance to gain your trust, stripping you bare of your insecurities, and teaching you to love those flaws. I want the real you, Angel. I want all of you, broken or whole baby, I want it all."

CHAPTER 10

*S*aint

10 years ago- Miami: night of second date

After making my declaration, I cleared my throat and took another gulp of my Hennessy. Waiting for her response left me anxious. Perfection wasn't something I sought after. Only fools searched for perfection. I wanted real; whether it was flawed or not. Whatever insecurities she stored internally were motivation to prove my true intentions to her. It was vital that she understand that damaged or not, I wanted her. In return, she'd have all of me.

Angel stood up and began walking around the table towards me. I pushed my seat back, anticipating what was to come. Her wide hips swaying towards had me in a hypnotic state. I couldn't pull my eyes from them. It wasn't until she straddled me that I looked up into her eyes. There was a mixture of emotions hidden in them. Lust. Pain. Uncertainty. Hope. Fear.

"Kiss me," she commanded. It wasn't a question. It was a clear demand. That's when I realized that I had lost my ability to tell her no. No part of me wanted to deny her. It was no longer an option that I had.

I leaned into her before taking her plump bottom lip into my mouth. I savored the taste of her mouth as our kiss deepened. With one hand on her waist and the other in her thick curly hair, I drew her closer into me. I held onto her as tightly as I could, hoping to feed the need that was burning inside of me. Hoping that her sweet saliva would drip down my throat and put out the fire that was threatening to burn me alive.

She pulled away, taking my breath and heart with her.

"Honesty. Can you give me that?" she asked.

Without any reluctance I answered, "Yes. Are you sure you want that?"

She had to be certain of what she was asking of me. Honesty wasn't the issue because I was a man of my word. I didn't get in the position I was in by being a snake. Complete honesty seemed like a good request until it was actually given. Some people just weren't built for it. If Angel wanted that, she had to be able to handle the reality that came along with it.

With her eyes glued to mine, I told her everything that I thought may have caused her to change her mind about wanting to take this path with me, "My full name is Saint Amad Baptiste. I'm stubborn and rude sometimes. I don't have a filter. When I feel it's for a good reason, I'm selfish as hell. I'm real heavy in the streets. I'm a boss and that means anything could happen."

As expected, her dark brown eyes grew as wide as saucers as she tried to remove herself from my grip. With both hands planted on her waist, I held her in place. Angel's reaction didn't surprise me. I didn't blatantly tell her I was the head of my own organization, but she understood what I said. She wanted honesty, so that's exactly what I was going to give to her. I expected the same in return. I continued, "You wanted honesty therefore that's what I'm going to give you at all times. I expect the same in return. Before you run away, be honest with me. Tell me why you are fighting what we both felt from the beginning. Why are you limiting my access to you? Is it because I saw right past all of that?" I took a deep breath before continuing, "Don't run from fate baby. You don't have to walk away from me. If you do, just know that I plan on catching you."

Her eyes lowered, and I halfway expected her to tell me she wasn't going to give me a chance. To my surprise, she opened up about her past. She and Harmony were brought to America from Haiti on the false pretense that they were coming for a better life. Their parents, who neither one of them could remember, gave them up in hopes that they would have all the opportunities that America had to offer. Instead they worked as "restavek" in the people's home that adopted them. Luckily, they were adopted together and were never separated. According to Angel, being together was the only thing that got them through years of abuse and cruelty.

She explained to me that a restavek translated to a child slave in English. They were children, often orphans, that lived with people that were most likely not related to them and did housework free of pay. Why pay for a maid when you could get a young and impressionable child to be a servant for free? It was a messed-up system but often happened when a family couldn't afford to properly take care of their children. Sometimes it was elitist in Haiti that took in parentless children. Sometimes it was foreigners that used being missionaries as a front to falsely adopt young children in Haiti.

"It was hell, Saint. I remember my mom filling me up with dreams of me becoming successful and going back to Haiti to help her. My aunt did the same with Harmony. Instead we were brought here, stripped of our identity, and worked from sunup to sundown. They would starve us and beat us every day. From the age of four to eighteen, I was beaten every single day."

Her head shook as she described the events of her past. Angel may have been young, but she had gone through more pain than most people. From having to go days without anything but water, to having to heal from broken bones. It was becoming clear why she had trust issues. She was promised a better life but in turn lost her home, parents, culture—everything. There wasn't any way I could give her any of that back. If there was a chance for me to go back in time and fix it all, I would've. That was impossible, so I chose to focus on what I had power to control. Her future. Our future together.

Listening responsively, I allowed her to expose her wounded heart for me to finally see. I wasn't going to try and fix it. She needed to get rid of it entirely for her own personal growth. As she expressed her pain in verbal form, I felt the heaviness of her spirit lightening up. If she was willing to deal with my profession, who was I to judge her for past she hadn't had any power to dictate.

The food that I had prepared four us was never eaten. The candles had longed burned out. The moon watched over us as it offered us our only source of light. We sat in the sand with her head in my lap. Angel and I spent five hours talking about our past and what led us to where we were today. From the first time since I met her, the uncertainty had disappeared from her eyes. The uncertainty was never about me or my intentions. It all had to do with not knowing what her life would become. She told me that she didn't have a real job because she was unable to get one. She never gave me the reason as to why she was unable to get a job, but she did what she could do; she braided hair. I appreciated the hustle in her.

"Is that something that you want to do long term? Do you want to eventually own a shop or something like that?" I asked. She didn't know it, but I was going to make sure she was set for the future she wanted. Whether she left Miami as just my friend or us working towards something more, her future would no longer be stuck in a limbo.

Angel yelled *hell no,* bringing us both to laughter. She then went on to explain that she braided hair because she was good at it. It was her only sure way of bringing in money and that was the main reason she did it. When I asked what she really wanted to do, she clarified that for the duration of her life she wanted to be a mother and a nurse. The idea of having children had never even crossed my mind. Not until she told me she felt that her true purpose was to be a loving mother to four children. She was dead serious, so I couldn't even laugh at how specific she was. It made me want to give her all that plus more.

"I vow to always protect you," I randomly said. Angel may have thought that I was only referring to protecting her heart. She couldn't have been more wrong. It was imperative that I protected every single part of her. I had to help her rebuild the parts of her that were stained by those that abused her, along with protecting the parts that she had yet to open to anyone.

As we left the beach, my spirit felt lighter. Not because I suddenly gained her trust. This wasn't fairytale, I was going to have to work towards that. It was because I could tell she was open to the possibility of trusting me. If she could put up with how straightforward I was, how could I not put in the work to gain her full trust?

———

It had been a long day having to deal with a shortage in the profit from two of our stash houses. That was Loco's job and he dropped the ball. Whenever he called me, he made it a point not to go over the details over the phone. He also felt the need to not mention it at the airport. It was the first time that had happened but that didn't matter to me. My livelihood wasn't built on making mistakes. Miami was new territory for me, which meant that I couldn't afford any slip-ups. He messed up in a major way. After fixing it, the natural thing to do was demote him. Amateur mistakes were for amateurs. I wasn't one of those, nor was I going to let someone make me look like one. After I was done with him, I called Jonas to have Dice come down to Miami. Dice was more solid than Loco had proven himself to be. Everyone around me had to be solid. By the time I was done, it was eight o'clock at night and I hadn't gotten any sleep.

Throughout the day, Angel and I texted. I stepped away twice to call her. It was hard being apart from her, knowing she was in Miami for me. I knew it was only a matter of time until we had the talk about the time restrictions my profession placed on me. She seemed to have understood but she was a woman. She needed quality time more than anything. If I couldn't offer that, losing her would be easier than keeping her. That wasn't something I wanted to happen. No, it was never going to happen.

As much I wanted to make another grand gesture for Angel, my body wouldn't let me. I had been up for over twenty-four hours and needed rest. Still wanting to spend time with her, I had a driver pick Angel up to bring her to my townhome in Coral Gables. I loved the neighborhood because it was far from the busyness of downtown Miami. Ma picked the neighborhood since she felt that if the possibility of having a family of my own ever presented itself, then it was a good neighborhood to raise children in. For the most part, I always listened to my mom. To appease her, I bought the townhome in Coral Gables with no hopes of upgrading to a house. At the time, creating a family of my own didn't seem possible. Now, maybe it could be a part of my future.

The driver called to inform me that he was ten minutes from my house just as the food and flowers I ordered, arrived. Having to deal with Loco's mess up meant that I had to once again, alter my original plans. She agreed to a night in with food and conversation, however her agreeance was consequent of several texts and a phone call to influence her decision. My appreciation was at an all-time high because I desperately needed a night of relaxation. With no sleep in almost two days, I wasn't good for much else than a night in.

The knock on the door grabbed my attention, forcing me to drag my tired body from the comfortable couch. Opening the door, my breathing suddenly stopped. I didn't care what anybody said, the beauty of a woman in her natural state was one that would forever be unmatched. No enhancements, just effortlessly her. That was what Angel presented me with—her.

She tugged at the bottom of the mustard yellow flare dress that stopped two inches above her knees. The spaghetti straps that held the dress on her shoulders, drew my attention to her bare arms. The center of her dress swathed her mid-section tightly. Her comfort level deteriorating the more my eyes refused to break its gaze from her. It wasn't merely her beauty; it was her energy. It was stained but innocent. It was unrefined and excellence enclosed in one. She was a contradiction standing before me in human form. We were a contradiction. A beautiful contradiction. Everything that wasn't supposed to be but was meant to be. Fate determined that, and it was the one thing I never went against. She may have tried to convince me to believe it would be hard for her to offer me her trust, but her energy told me otherwise.

"Are you going to bring your pretty ass inside or do I have to carry you in?" She smiled, melting my apprehension away.

"You cannot pick me up. In case you haven't noticed, I am nowhere close to a size six," she said.

Angel was definitely not a size six. If I had to guess, I would say she was a fourteen. She was full-figured and shapely. My eyes ran across her body in admiration before I lifted her in my arms bridal style. I had a point to prove. After tonight, she was going to stop doubting me. As I carried her to the brown leather couch, she squirmed in my arms. Angel didn't know but she met my exact preference. Her body was amazing and when the time was right, I would show her just how much I adored each curve on her stunningly made body.

Sitting her down on the couch, I went into the kitchen to retrieve the food and flowers. When I returned, I found her in the same spot I left her in. Her hands laid against her voluptuous thighs with her dress moving further up, exposing more than what I saw earlier. Naturally, my body reacted as you would expect it to. I quickly shook those thoughts out of my mind. My spirit wasn't ready to be tied to hers, knowing that we both needed to trust one another.

She turned to look at me when she felt my presence and said, "I'm not having sex with you."

I shouldn't have been surprise by her declaration but that didn't stop it from feeling as if someone punched me directly in my chest. Whenever I called her, I made it clear that sex was not why I wanted her to come over. I made it crystal clear that I hadn't slept in over twenty-four hours but wanted to give her the quality time she deserved. It took everything in me not to say forget it and call a driver to take her back to the hotel. The Saint that everyone knew, would've done exactly that. The one that she had recently introduced me to, chose to handle the situation differently.

Thoughts of how to word what I wanted to say to convey my point, ran through my head. She had to stop second-guessing me. She had to stop doubting my words. I fully understood her past and her lack of trust, but I also saw the internal battle she was fighting. Angel knew she could trust me, but she was fighting it with everything she had. The moment she felt herself losing, she said some off the wall shit.

After I sat the food and flowers on the mahogany coffee table in front of us, I sat next to her making sure to keep a couple of inches in between us. With my elbows on my knees and hands clasped together, I did my best to control my breathing. I didn't even bother looking in her direction. "Did I tell you that we were going to have sex, or did I specifically say that I had no intentions of us having sex anytime soon?"

"You're wearing only basketball shorts with all of your tattoos showing. If sex wasn't on your mind, then you wouldn't be hard right now," she said with her eyes briefly shifting towards my growing manhood.

I shook my head at how silly she sounded before saying,

"I never said sex wasn't on my mind. Of course, it is. I am human and you are very attractive. The reason I'm only wearing basketball shorts is because I'm relaxed in my home. Do you want me to put a shirt on? Will that make you more comfortable?"

She bit on her bottom lip and instead of waiting for her to answer, I went up the stairs to my bedroom to retrieve a plain white shirt and a pair of jeans. Once I finished putting them on, I went back downstairs. She still hadn't moved an inch.

"Do you need me to put on shoes too or are my socks ok?" I asked.

A smirk crept across her gorgeously carved face, "Can you put on shoes, too?"

"Miss Pecan stop playing with me." I sunk into the couch, feeling her burn a hole into the side of my face.

"What did you just call me?" Turning to face her, I found that her eyes displayed a hint of jealousy.

"Relax. Before you told me your name, that's what I called you. Your skin complexion reminds me of pecans."

She nodded her head and then said, "Mr. Chocolate."

"What?"

"That's what I called you because of your skin complexion." Her statement allowed the tension to begin evaporating from the room.

That was how all of our interactions went. It was beginning to bother me because she would create the tension, when there wasn't a reason for it. She tried her hardest to prevent what was happening naturally and I couldn't help but to laugh out loud. It was a hearty laugh that originated from my diaphragm. It was comical how hard she tried to hinder what had already happened. She was my person. Mine. Without her knowledge, she gave me the desire to give her everything: safety, security, love, honesty, and all of my trust. Angel made me want to give her a family. Most importantly, she had me wanting to have a family for me.

"Angel, what do I have to do get you to stop fighting me?"

"I just need time," she said it almost as if she believed it.

"No, you don't need time. You have that already. I'm not asking you to marry me today. I'm asking you to stop fighting this. Stop building a wall up every time we are together, knowing that I will do everything possible to break it down. I want you Angel. Believe me when I say nothing will change that, but you have to let things happen how they are meant to. Please babe."

She didn't answer me with her words like I had expected her to. Instead, she laid her forehead on mine, prompting both of our eyes to close simultaneously while allowing our silence to make the declaration of our hearts. She may have not said it, but I felt it. Her heart was telling me that it was not the one putting up a fight, logic was. Angel wasn't going to stop fighting against our connection. That's why she couldn't answer verbally. She didn't want to lie by answering yes, nor did she want to say no because that only meant there was a possibility of me no longer having the will to pursue her.

"Let's eat," I said, breaking our connection. She only had tonight, and one full day left in Miami. I wasn't going to let any negativity ruin it.

She simply nodded her head and grabbed the to-go box from the table. Angel opened up the box and her mouth fell open. Inside of her plate was red beans and rice, red snapper fish drenched in a savory tomato-based stew, and fried plantains.

"Saint," she said in a soft voice. She bit her bottom lip in an attempt to not give in to the smirk that was threatening to take over her face.

When she told me about how she had lost her culture, my plan was to give her a piece of it by taking her and Harmony to Little Haiti to experience the culture. My initial plan was to take them to Haiti, but I had no idea if either had a valid passport with them, therefore Little Haiti made more sense. The day escaped from me due to work, so the last resort was to get her authentic Haitian food as well Haiti's unofficial flower, the hibiscus flower. I took the flower from the coffee table and explained to her the significance of them. Her eyes expressed the gratitude that she was unable to voice. This time our food didn't go to waste. At least hers didn't, I spent more time watching her enjoying her meal than I spent eating my own.

From there, the conversation began to flow smoothly. She was hesitant to ask why I sold drugs. It was hard to answer that question because I didn't have a reason other than I wanted to. I promised her honesty, so I explained it to her the best that I could.

"It was easy and fast money which attracted me to it. My parents worked hard to make ends meet as immigrants, but I wanted better for us. When I was fifteen, my best friend, Jonas and I would watch out for the police for the local dealers. All the money we made, we kept at Jonas' house. Ma was nosy, and I didn't need her finding it. His father was still in Haiti, so his mom worked two jobs to take care of him and his brother. She was barely home."

"How did you get to where you are now if you started off watching out for the cops?" she asked. Her head was in my lap while I sat back on the couch. Rubbing my fingers through her tresses, I searched her eyes only to find compassion and curiosity.

Not having discovered a sign judgment, I went on to explain that by the age of twenty-one, we had enough saved up between the two of us to start our own small organization. We were smart though. We didn't sell on the corners because they were already taken. We wanted to remain low key as well as, not getting into a market that was already over-saturated. We went to Brentwood, Franklin, and the Mount Juliet area of Tennessee. After doing that for a year, just the two of us, we began building a team. Only the first two people on our team knew who we were; Dice and Legend. The two were cousins and didn't mind being the face while Jonas and I were the bosses. Having a reputation in the streets wasn't of value to me. Those that needed to know who I was, knew. The ones that needed to know the power that my name held, did. My face didn't have to be shown for that to happen. The power and respect were all that mattered.

After I was done, Angel went on to reveal more about her and Harmony's relationship. The two were more like sisters than cousins. She clarified to me that the people that adopted her and Harmony on false pretenses, gave them the option to leave once they turned eighteen. Harmony turned eighteen before she did but didn't want to leave her. She practically had to beg her to leave. They hatched a plan for Harmony to leave and when she was somewhat stable, Angel would go to wherever she was as soon she turned eighteen. Angel didn't go into detail about certain parts of her story, but I wasn't going to push it. When she wanted me to know it all, she would tell me. After a few hours, sleep began demanding to take over my body.

"Let me take you back to the hotel babe." I rubbed my hand over my head before getting up from the couch to go back to the kitchen. I returned with two food containers to find her standing by the door.

"What are these for?" she asked, pointing at the food containers in my hand.

"What does it look like?"

She rolled her eyes. "Smart ass."

"Pot calling the kettle black baby but since I'm not as rude as you, I'm going to answer your question. It's Haitian food. One for you and one for Harmony. I'm sure the room service is good, but this is better."

Angel smiled as she hurried over to me. Caressing my left arm, she rested her head on my chest.

I pulled her head back by her thick curls and planted a kiss on her inviting lips. "When I get done handling business in the morning, I'll pick the both of you up for a day out."

She nodded her head and but didn't say anything. I was a lot to take in and when the time was right, Angel would have no choice but to take in all of me.

CHAPTER 11

*A*ngel
10 years ago-Day 2 in Miami

"Did you tell him everything?"

It was our second full day in Miami, but technically our third day. Harmony and I had just finished getting dressed, waiting for Saint to pick us up for a day out in the city. Harmony was waiting up for me when Saint dropped me off at one in the morning. We stayed up for a couple of hours eating and conversing about everything that had been transpiring between Saint and me. She was team Saint from the beginning but him buying us Haitian food solidified it. He gave us a piece of our culture that we'd been missing. Saint provided us with a small part of who we were, before we both were stripped of our identities.

"Not everything, just some of it," I answered.

"Why didn't you tell him everything?"

I stood up from my bed and began pacing the floor back and forth, chewing the inside of my right cheek to keep me calm. There was no way I could tell Saint all of my past. He knew the major parts that led to my trust issues. "Because none of it matters. He knows the important stuff."

"So, let me get this right. You don't think that you being here due to a phony adoption process is important? Or the fact that you are literally hiding from your ex because you ran away from him?"

Feeling my emotions starting to get the best of me, I returned to join her at the edge of her bed. She may have thought that it wise to tell Saint all of those things, but I didn't. Those were parts of my life that I was trying my hardest to detach from. How would he not walk away from me when I was ready to walk away from myself? I couldn't have that, so I was going to make sure I was the one that walked away when I got back to Nashville.

I was constantly reminded of my illegal status in America because I wasn't able to get a real job or attend school. It made me angry to think that those people took us from our family and didn't even bother giving us real documentation to function. Harmony got lucky and found someone to give her a green card. She was still indebted to him and gave him most of the money she made from working part-time at the store. He was actually the one that introduced me to my ex, thinking he would do the same for me. That was not the case at all, he had other plans. Harmony apologized several times for having him introduce me to him but neither of us would've guessed that he was the devil in disguise.

"He knows I'm here because of a fake adoption."

"Let me rephrase that since you aren't grasping what I'm saying. You have to tell him that you're here illegally, Angel. He might help you get your papers."

I shot up from the bed, feeling anger travel up my body

and bursting from inside of me. "You are crazy! I'm not asking him for that."

"Why not?" Harmony sat on the bed calmly, waiting for me to answer her hundredth question of the day.

There wasn't a reason for me to answer because she should've known the answer. I couldn't run the risk of Saint thinking I was using him to become legal. On top of that, there was my crazy ex, Derrick. He presented himself as councilman during the day to the public but at night, he was someone different. No one would've guessed that he was involved in a drug and prostitution ring. Putting all of that on Saint wasn't an option at all. That's why I couldn't go further with him. Everything about Saint told me he would do anything in his power to make sure I was in a good place mentally, physically, and spiritually. He didn't deserve to deal with my bullshit-filled luggage. A heart as pure and as genuine as his deserved one that wasn't riddled with the pain of it's past.

"He doesn't need all of the extra baggage I come with."

"Saint is asking for it though. It's not like you are giving it to him, it's him taking it from you. That's what men do, Angel. No real man will allow you to go through life alone. I see that clear as day. Why can't you?"

Why couldn't I see that? Maybe it was because for so long, I had to think that way. Possibly it was because I felt that Saint was too good for me. It could've been because I didn't earn anything good in this life. When you only knew bad, it was hard to believe you deserved good. And Saint was better than good. He was everything that love represented. The possibility of having that shuddered my belief in not being worthy of love. So much so that my fear of it ending badly, tempted me to never truly start it.

Thankfully before she could further press the issue,

there was a knock on the door. I left her on the bed and went to open it. Saint appeared wearing black jeans and a simple dark gray V-neck shirt. His tattoos dancing against his bare arms peeked at me, begging me to run my hands across the smooth surface that they decorated so beautifully. He pulled me into a tight hug, granting me access to immerse myself in his manly scent, his strength—all of him. With eyes closed, I visualized the possibility of a future for us with everything that he was offering me. Just as much it seemed possible, it seemed just as impossible. I had to protect his heart even if he didn't think it needed protecting.

The three of us left the hotel and headed to a building that had an industrial kitchen. He prepared brunch for the three of us to enjoy. The food was amazing. The ham and spinach omelet were the best I ever had. It put Arizona's Diner's omelet to shame.

"Saint this food is so good," Harmony said. The way she was stuffing her face, there wasn't any denying that she expressed exactly how she felt.

"That is just some slight work. Wait until mine and Angel's engagement party, I'll show you what real cooking is," he responded, his strong dark chocolate face beaming with pride as he winked at me.

My temperature started rising as I began to blush. The rush I was feeling was quickly followed by pain knowing that after I left Miami, I would never see him again. Saint was prideful, there was no way that he would come after me if I fully denied him access to me. The past few days I was cautious, but I always let him in. With us being miles apart, I wouldn't want the risk of being vulnerable to him.

He let out a loud gasp and clutched his chest. "What? Angel is speechless? How often does that happen?"

Rolling my eyes at him, I told Harmony to shut up

because she was almost on the floor due to laughing hysterically. He was not that funny. After we were done, Saint called someone to clean up for him. He then took us to downtown Little Haiti, bringing so much joy to Harmony and me. Haitian music filled the air. The creole language poured from the tip of the native speakers' tongues and graced my heart. The streets were flooded with some of the most vibrant people I ever had the privilege to witness. My heart was heavy and full to have been able to experience a part of what was taken from me. Saint had essentially given Harmony and I a piece of our true identity back. In the few short days that I'd know him, he'd done everything in his power to ensure I was aware of what he wanted from us being together. But him doing this for Harmony was another level of thoughtfulness that I had yet to experience from anyone.

I had no idea how my heart would take me removing her from him his grasp, but she would have to deal with the pain. A pain that both of us would have to share. It was best for him for it to end that way. With my life came too much uncertainty. Uncertainty that I wasn't willing to put him through. Not having legal status and hiding from my ex were two things that were bound to run anyone away. It was best for me to walk away because I couldn't bare the pain of falling and him leaving. It was best for him to not fall completely, then to fall and find out the complications that came along with it.

Trust played the biggest factor because I didn't trust him enough to tell him everything. Hell, it surprised the hell out of me when I told him about the adoption. He was trusting in our connection to guide him, while I was using my fear to lead me down a path of loneliness. We were headed in two directions and he didn't know it. It was for the best. At least, that's what I was telling myself every minute that I spent with him.

Once we left Little Haiti, he took us to the mall to shop. Initially, I didn't want to get anything. It only made sense not to because the end of whatever we were, would come as soon as I boarded the plane tomorrow morning. Harmony on the other hand, didn't have to be told twice. She enjoyed every bit of Saint spoiling us. The credit card he gave us was still with me. Whenever I tried to give it back, he refused. According to him, with his card, he could guarantee that I wouldn't lack anything when I went back to Nashville.

While Harmony was literally skipping around the store picking out clothes for the both of us, Saint pulled me to the closest bench outside of the store with worry painted on his face. *His face.* God, I would miss his handsome face.

He sat me down first. Then he kneeled in front of me, humbling himself before me. With my hands in his, he began to break me down. "Your vibe has been off since we left breakfast baby. I'm starting to have a love-hate relationship with being able to feel what you feel." He chuckled before continuing, "How is your spirit feeling? What do I need to do?"

How was my spirit feeling? He couldn't have possibly known the significance of that question. How could he? My spirit determined my mood. If it was light, my mood was light. I was free. If it was heavy, then I lost focus and became emotionally drained. I fought it the hardest today because he went over and beyond for not only me, but Harmony as well. The realization of him giving himself to me weighed me down. Just when I thought I was doing a good job at masking it, he saw right through it.

"You are too good for me Saint."

Letting my hand go, he rubbed his hand across his

freshly cut hair. I chewed on the inside of my right cheek, waiting for him to respond. He returned my hands back into his, this time holding them tighter. Squeezing them, possibly hoping to squeeze some sense back into me.

"Angel please don't take this the wrong way baby but I'm about to get real blunt with you. Can you handle that?"

I nodded my head for him to continue, "You aren't stupid. You aren't crazy but that's exactly how you sound right now." I wanted to smile so badly because he even in his seriousness, he was attempting to lighten up the mood. Fighting my laughter, I listened carefully to every single word he spoke into me, in hopes that it would take away all of my doubts and fears.

"You're the one that is too good for me. I don't deserve to have a heart as fragile as yours because I have no idea how to handle it with care. I am going to let this connection that I feel with you be my blueprint. Don't run away from me please, I am begging you. That need for me that I see in your eyes, I have that same need in my heart, babe."

Saint brought my hands to his chest, affording me the honor to feel the rhythm of his heart, "It's yours, Ang. It hasn't ever belonged to any other woman besides my Ma. From today forward, you come first, you will be my first and only wife, the mother of my four children, and everything else that you want. I will be your protector, supporter, provider, husband, and father to your four children. We will not fall in love. Falling is an accident. We are no accident."

He brought my hands to his soft lips, kissed it once, "We are meant to be." *Kiss.* "We will grow in love." *Kiss.* "We will learn to trust each other fully." *Kiss.* "We will become one."

Taking my bottom lip in between his honied lips, he made love to my mouth. My soul left my body, only returning to shame me for wanting to part ways with her mate. She may have not understood it, but I had to put Saint's heart before mine. He trusted me with it and the only way to protect it was leaving him with it and as far away from me as possible.

CHAPTER 12

*S*aint

10 years ago- 1 week later

She lied to me. She had me at my most vulnerable state and chose to lie to me. Some might've viewed it as her changing her mind, but I didn't. Let your yes, be your yes and your no, be your no. Don't switch up. Never allow someone to envision a future that you both created together to then take the decision solely upon themselves to destroy it. Angel allowed fear to consume her and damage what we should've been working towards fixing together.

Her and Harmony had spent the entire day with me. The day was a much-needed refresher and confirmed everything that I felt to be true. She was the one for me. She was my better half. Angel helped me stay level-headed in her presence. She granted me access to be exposed for the first time, only to turn around and shit on me. Any woman would've gladly taken everything that I was offering to Angel. Thing was, my everything was only meant to be given to Angel. That brought pain along with and its companion—anger.

It had been a week since she returned to Nashville. The first four days I texted and called her nonstop; begging and pleading with her to starve whatever it was feeding her fear. She didn't block my number, she read every single text I sent to her. I was damn near positive she listened to the ten voicemails I left for her. On day five, I called Harmony. Not hearing from Angel was killing me. Even though I was hurting, I had to find a way to make sure she was ok. That her spirit was at peace with her foolish decision. My call went straight to voicemail. Angel had to have blocked my number on her phone because Harmony wouldn't have. She was nowhere near as stubborn or guarded as Angel was.

Day six, my fury consumed me. It was fuck her and every moment we spent together. Fuck her fear and her soiled heart. Fuck the possibility of us having a family together. Fuck me thinking that I could retire and have everything that my vivid dreams deceived me into believing would be a reality.

Day seven, I was back in Nashville. On my way to her apartment for her to tell me she didn't want me, to my face. She didn't get to cower away in Nashville while I dealt with the effects of her absence. She wanted to pull away, she was going to see what she caused.

She had no idea, but I had eyes on her. Jonas had someone watch every move she made. I couldn't run the risk of someone else holding my place in her life. Without me knowing, she left the credit card I gave her, on the floor. At first, it seemed that it might've fell out but when my calls and texts went unanswered, I knew she did that shit on purpose. To guarantee she was taken cared of financially, I made sure to build up her clientele myself. She was only charging fifty dollars per head. Her talent and livelihood were worth more than that. Each day she would get five clients that I referred, unbeknownst to her. They would each get their hair braided and offered her a nothing smaller than a fifty-dollar tip. However, today I made sure she didn't have any. Even though my mind said fuck her and what she had done. My heart was pushing me towards her just as it had done the night of the house party.

Walking up to the front door, I took a deep breath. I had vowed to myself that I would never raise my voice at her, or to her. My built-up frustration said otherwise. I raised my balled-up fist to the door and knocked twice. The sound of footsteps traveled to my ears from the other side of the door followed by stillness. "Angel, open up."

She unlocked the door before taking what felt like an eternity to open it. Unable to wait for her to open it completely, I pushed myself inside and closed the door behind me. The hurt I felt washed away the moment I saw her red eyes and disheveled appearance. Her curly hair was all over her head. Her body draped in one of my black t-shirts and a pair of pink boy shorts, looked weak. My eyes drifted to her bare thighs and roamed up her body, until our eyes connected for the first time in seven days. Just like that. One second. That's all it took for my anger towards her to vanish.

"Where's Harmony?"

"She's not here," she answered.

Rage was replaced with defeat. My shoulders dropped as did my head. Refusing to let her energy take control of mine and make me weak to her again, I walked over to the one couch that was in the living room. It was my first time in her apartment. It was small but homey. The kitchen and living room put together were the size of just my living room. I looked down the hallway to notice that there were only two doors. The apartment was extremely clean even though the furniture wasn't up to date.

"Why did you do it?" I asked once I was able to get my thoughts together. That was the only explanation she had to give me. If she didn't value our bond enough, it was up to me to do it for the both of us. If she could give me a valid reason, then I would walk away knowing that love was not in my future. Accepting that appeared easy because until her, I had never thought love was for me. She gave it to me; it was only right she stripped me of it.

She walked around and kneeled in front of me. This wasn't how I imagined everything would happen. Whenever I played it in my head, this was not what came to mind. She chewed on the inside of her right cheek—her tell.

"I'm so sorry Saint," she whispered while looking down. This was my first time being in this position, and I was lost with no clear direction on where to go. Yes, a part wanted me to just walk away from her and her sorry. Sorry didn't mean shit to me. It couldn't rewind time nor take away the aching she created for the both of us.

However, the important part of me wanted to pull her into my arms more than anything. I wanted to prove to her that we weren't merely a coincidence of two souls colliding. Her and I were destined for one another. We both had a past but wanted better for the future. It was designed for us to give that to one another. To be one another's journey to a brighter future.

"What are you sorry for?" In order for me to get through to her, I couldn't be soft. Begging her had already transpired and she left me for seven whole days.

She looked up at me as she stood to her feet. She paced the small living room back and forth before stopping to face me. "You were right. This week apart proved that to me."

"Right about what exactly?" I had done most of the talking, the begging, and convincing. Ang needed to see that shit on her own. This was her opportunity to tell me what I was right about and why the hell she was running from something she couldn't deny.

"You and I are meant to be, but I am damaged. I don't know if I can love and trust you the way you deserve. That's not fair to you or your heart."

"Stop saying that. Stop saying you don't deserve me. Stop denying what you feel for me. Why can't you try and trust me? Trust takes time to build but you rather run away than give me that. Don't you think I deserve time?" I quickly jumped to my feet. Within two seconds, I was in her face. She no longer was going to get a chance to run away.

She didn't jump back. She didn't back down. Instead, Angel looked into my eyes and said, "You deserve everything that you desire from me."

My head started spinning. Feeling myself get lightheaded, I left her standing in the center of the room and made my way towards the front door. I needed to get the fuck away from her. She was making me go crazy.

"You came all the way to Nashville to walk away?"

That question sent my fury to a level that I didn't recognize. My line of work didn't even stress me out to the point where I lost all control. Against my better judgment I responded, "Your young ass is really confused, and I don't have the time for it. You were told what I wanted from you and what I'd give in return. Don't make it seem like I'm the one walking away. Angel, you walked away from me. What did I get from opening up to you? Don't worry, I'll answer for you. I got shitted on."

She rushed over to me, "You got my heart!"

"You didn't have control over that because you didn't give it to me. It was mine to have. What I want is your trust and honesty."

"My past..."

Cutting her off I said, "Babe, please don't take this the wrong way because I mean this with the upmost respect," I paused before continuing, "but fuck your past!"

My voice heightened more than I wanted to. The excuse of her past wasn't cutting it anymore. It didn't impact the future. Nothing from her past made me not want to be with her. No matter how many times I told her that, she still had it stuck in her head that it did.

She shook her head and said, "You don't get it."

That was the only flaw she had shown me. She didn't want me to me make assumptions about her, yet she always made them of me. She asked for honesty but reciprocated it with secrecy. What I offered to her didn't seem like it was enough, but it was all I had to give. If it wasn't enough for her, fuck it. This love shit may have not been for me after all. I gave it a fair shot, but she provided it with inconsistency. The streets never offered me that, so the plan to eventually leave it to give her everything she wanted, disappeared from every corner of my mind even though it would be forever inscribed in my heart. The back and forth shit wasn't for me and it never would be. Not even Angel could make me change that.

"Let me explain Saint," she pleaded with me. It was a little too late for that. Angel ignoring me for a week didn't even mess it up. It was her acting as if I was the one that gave up when she never gave me a chance to begin with.

"Ain't shit to explain, Angel. What do you have to tell me? You think I don't know about the falsified documents to bring you to America? That you're technically here illegally and that's the reason you can't get real employment and go to school. Or you don't think I know about your bitch ass ex, Derrick?"

Angel's eyes grew wide and then became filled with anger. Her voice was so loud that it shook me, "You knew this whole time!"

"Only after you left, and you know what? None of that shit mattered then, now, and it sure as hell wouldn't have matter when you became my wife."

I did my research on Angel. Granted our connection was strong but shaking off the feeling that she was hiding something, was impossible to do. It didn't take a genius to figure out what her adoptive parents had done was illegal. They created fake documents to smuggle her and Harmony into the country. They home schooled them, so that they were able to read and write but weren't allowed to attend regular school. It wasn't until Harmony turned eighteen, did they find out that they were both illegal. Fortunately for Harmony, she found someone to give her a green card, Councilman Samuel Edwards. It came at one price—her virginity.

To my knowledge, she gave it to him. She was desperate and desperation made people do things they wouldn't normally do. After he defiled her, he kept his end of the deal, married her but later requested that she gave him five thousand dollars for him not to cancel it. She was giving him half of her check every time she got paid. He was a greedy motherfucker because he had money. He was exercising his power over her. Fuck nigga shit.

When Angel turned eighteen a year later, Harmony tried to do the same thing with her as well with Samuel's brother, Councilman Derrick Edwards. Again, I understood because that was their only option. Being an immigrant myself, I knew the importance of being legal in America. There's was a different circumstance because they didn't know anything about Haiti or their family. If they were deported, they would literally have nowhere to go. America was the only place they had the possibility of surviving.

Angel's terms were a bit different then Harmony. Harmony left Boston and moved to Nashville with the promise of paying him as soon as she had a job. She paid him promptly every two weeks, so he didn't have a reason to look for her. He had a fiancée and Harmony was a temptation that he knew that he wouldn't be able to resist. Nigga had a fiancée and still married Harmony. Apparently, chocolate pussy was the white man's weakness.

Derrick wasn't committed to anyone, so he wanted Angel to be his live-in girlfriend. She went from being his girlfriend, to his punching bag, then a personal sex slave and then a sex slave to one of friends. After that, the physical abuse only got worse. One day he left some money out, she took a couple of hundred, and left to join Harmony. She went into hiding because he had people looking for her. All of that information wasn't hard to find since both of them had their hands in the drug game. Regrettably for them, my reach was longer.

"How did you find out? Saint, please, don't tell me you know everything." She started shaking violently. Pools of tears fled from her dark brown eyes and formed a trail down to her plump lips. Shame stamped all across her beautiful face.

Even though I was furious with her for flipping the table on me, I couldn't stand seeing her the way she was. I picked her up bridal style and carried her away from the door and back to the couch. Sitting her down, I wrapped my arms around her tightly. Angel cried for a minute before gathering herself. She took a deep breath and for the first time, she poured her soul into me.

"I did what thought was best. If I left, your pride wouldn't let you come after me. Clearly, I was wrong." She smiled at me and I reciprocated the gesture. She continued, "I didn't want to burden you or have you think I wanted a green card from you. My past might say otherwise but this isn't that."

I didn't have to hear it from her voice for me to recognize that this wasn't that. Angel was a genuine soul. Her past was tarnished, her heart was guarded, her trust was almost impenetrable, but her soul, it remained pure. Angel went on to explain her version of the story that I had already gotten from her white adoptive parents, the Edwards brothers, and Derrick's friend. There wasn't any derivation from the stories I originally heard. With Mac's help, it was easy to find all of them. They had to pay for everything single thing she had gone through. The physical pain, all of the mental agony, I made sure the five of them felt it. Ten years in the game, I had yet to catch any bodies. We had men for that. Yet, my growing feelings for Angel led me to catching my first, second, third, fourth, and fifth all in one night.

We stressed the importance of honesty but this one thing I wasn't able to tell her. If it were ever to come back on me, she couldn't be implemented. I had to make sure of that. It was a secret that would be buried with me when it was my time to go. That was just the way it had to be.

"How were you able to find all of this out?" she asked after she finished her story.

"I told you before, Angel. I'm a boss. With the help of a friend, I was able to find out everything, even information on you and Harmony's birth parents. When you're ready and able, I can take you both to them."

She hopped into my lap, straddling me only the way that she could and sat her fat ass directly on my risen manhood. "What did I do to deserve you?" she asked.

"Attend a whack ass house party." She smiled wildly as she stared at my lips. Licking my lips, I granted her wish to what her eyes requested but lips didn't speak. I slipped my right hand under my shirt that she was wearing and grazed her soft skin with just my fingertips.

"You should've answered the phone if you missed me, baby," I said. She moaned loudly in response. I continued, "My hand against your skin feels better than my shirt doesn't it, babe?"

Again, she moaned in response. "I can't hear you," I groaned as I took her right breast into my mouth. She moaned louder, causing my manhood to grow harder.

I removed my mouth from her breast and twirled my tongue around her enlarged nipple. Pulling away I said, "You made me suffer for seven days. I don't know if I should punish you for that or reward you for coming to your senses."

Pulling away from her, I waited for her response. With desire in her eyes and lust dripping from her tongue, she answered, "Punish me."

With one swift movement, I flipped her on her back atop of the couch. I removed her panties that were already stained by her honied nectar. She removed my shirt that had her body wrongfully hidden from me as I removed all of my clothing.

I watched as she spread her legs, granting me access to her canal. It was glistening, drawing me in willingly. Placing the head at her opening, I hesitated. Neither of us planned for this. I didn't bring any protection, but I didn't want to stop either. "I don't have any condoms," I stated, hopeful she was on birth control. She was clean, I checked so I wasn't worried about that. My greatest fear was having children while I was still in the game.

"I'm not on birth control." My heart sunk a little, but my body didn't move. Angel continued, "but I'm not ovulating."

The moment the last word fled from her lips, my manhood entered inside of her. Her warmth tethered the soul tie that was destined to happen the night we met one another. She whimpered with each stroke, her moans matching my groans. The tightness of her walls enclosed me in, refusing to let go. Plunging harder into her pond, she begged me to go deeper. I was a good listener so as a result, I went faster, deeper, and harder. Her body shook as she and I reached our peak the same time. With me releasing inside of her, we came together as we became one.

We laid on the couch with me inside of her, allowing our heartbeats to be the only thing heard amongst us. Not wanting to detach from our first real physical connection, I remained inside of her. Angel was the one to break the silence that incased us.

"Three months."

"Three months for what?" I asked.

"I asked you for time, remember? Please Saint, I'm asking you to give me three months. Just three months to make sure this is what you want. Three months to grow in love, three months to build trust, and three months evolve more into becoming one. After three months, if you are still as sure as you are right now, I'll move to Miami."

"If I would've known all it would take was these good strokes that I just delivered to get you to agree to give me a real chance, I would've given them to you right there on the porch."

She slapped my arm and giggled, but I was dead serious. "As amazing as your strokes are and they are amazing, they have nothing to do with it. I feel more like myself with you than when I am by myself. If that makes sense."

"It does," I answered while still inside of her. I continued, "Three months baby." She kissed my lips and I decided to reward her for the second round.

CHAPTER 13

*A*ngel
Present day

Three weeks had passed since Saint and I had our conversation about having another baby. Between work and planning for the twins' birthday party in a few days, the topic hadn't come up again. Eventually, I would have to tell him. There wasn't any escaping that. I was just trying to find the best way to lessen the impact. We worked really hard to build trust in our relationship. It was more than me going behind his back to do something. It was also the fact that I'd been holding on to the secret for over a year. On top of that, if he were to find out that I told Ladi and Ashley before him, he was really going to lose it. Since entering a committed relationship, whenever we had our disagreements, he never raised his voice at me. I didn't see that happening when I told him. It was just hard because I knew my need to protect him would only bring him heartache, the same way it did ten years ago. I almost lost him then. A part of me knew that it wouldn't happen but then again, there was still that small possibility that his emotions would get the best of him. Albeit small, it was still a possibility. I would just have to deal with the consequences when they came. For right now, I was going to put my focus into Heaven and SJ's party and deal with it later.

Monica and I usually planned the twins' birthday together. Despite Saint having a strong dislike for her, he appreciated the love she showed to our children. Our friendship began six years ago. She was working at a grocery store that I was grocery shopping at. It was a weird encounter. I was going through her line and she randomly said something about my hair. At the time it was dyed burgundy. We had a friendly encounter every time I went through her line from then on. Six months after that, we saw each other at one of my favorite brunch spots in South Beach. I invited her to join me and we slowly became close associates. Trust had always been hard for me because the people in my past always had an ulterior motive. One that was never in my best interest. Harmony and Saint were the exceptions, until he introduced me to his family. My trust issues caused our friendship to develop slowly. It wasn't until about three years ago that I considered her my best friend. She was my only friend, until I met Ladi and Ashley. I didn't have much faith in anyone else. With everyone except my husband, there was a limit to my trust in them and it could easily be taken away.

Monica gained my trust to the point that when she told me she was feeling my brother-in-law after his break-up with his ex, Sasha, I got the two together. It was one of my biggest regrets. It showed me a side of her that I hadn't seen before. That was also the moment Saint's distain for her began. He really liked Monica at first and was happy I met someone I could call a friend in Miami. It took a long time but making a friend was growth for me and he loved seeing my growth more than anything.

At first everything was cool between Ace and her. Then she started expecting him to do everything for her. Both Saint and Ace believed in being providers and when Monica saw that, she made sure to take full advantage. A week after their first date, she quit her job. Then she gave Ace a sob story about how she got fired and he believed it. Shoot, I believed it and I knew the truth, so I couldn't judge him for believing her. I only found out because when I went back to the grocery store, I overheard her coworkers talking about her quitting because she got a new man to take care of her. When I confronted her about it, she didn't deny or confirm it. She kind of brushed it off. Of course, I told Saint; he lost it and that was when his detestation of her began. Her and Ace broke things off after she fought his ex. Sasha was out right crazy and manipulative, so him going from that to Monica was not an improvement. At first, I really thought she was, but certain situations brought out different sides out in people. Monica proved that. Like I said before, she wasn't a bad person, but she was not the best person.

Her and I agreed to meet at what became our favorite brunch spot, to finalize the details of the party. Heaven wanted a PJ Masks themed party. It was hers and SJ's favorite show. Once she told Saint what they wanted, nobody else's opinion matter. If SJ wanted another theme, then Saint would've made it a double themed party, but he didn't. He catered to Heaven just like his father. Although, SJ was undoubtably a mama's boy, I envied the connection that he and SJ shared. I would never tell Saint though. It enjoyed watching him walk around the house when SJ went into full mama's boy mode too much.

"I cannot believe the twins are turning four years old," Monica said in between bites of her food.

"Me either. They're going to start pre-K this year and I'm not ready for it."

"I'm surprised Saint hasn't tried to get you pregnant again. That's all the two of you do, have babies." She giggled before putting another forkful of eggs into her mouth

Monica only knew about one of my miscarriages because she was there when it happened. It happened two months before Saint and I conceived Miracle. She knew how much having a family meant to me, so I didn't take her words to heart.

I laughed it off and changed the subject to avoid the her asking questions. "The twins are so excited for this party. I can't wait for them to see everything."

"You know as long as Heaven is happy, Saint Jr. will be happy," she stated. It wasn't a lie. Everyone knew that to keep SJ happy, you had to make sure Heaven was happy.

"He's just like his damn father," I said while shaking my head.

"I have a question to ask but you have to promise that before you say no, you'll hear me out."

She should've never said that. If she had to offer up a disclaimer, then the answer would definitely be no. I didn't need to hear her out to know what my answer would be. "Go ahead."

She took a deep breath, released it, and asked, "Are Ace and Ladi going to be there?"

It took everything in me not to fall over laughing. Not being able to fathom why she would ask such an obvious question, I said, "Mon, that's their uncle and aunt. I shouldn't have to tell you for you to know that they will be there. That's a presumption you could've made all on your own."

The jealousy in her eyes intensified. In some way, I did feel bad for her, but she did it to herself. Nobody told her to fight Ace's ex to prove a point. Absolutely no one told her to ignore him for a month when he called her multiple times to apologize for something that was out of his control. She made those choices, nobody but her.

"I figured that but wanted to make sure. They know I'm going to be there right?"

"Yeah, they know." Monica's eyes lit up like Christmas lights, but I didn't understand why. Ace and Ladi were in their own little world of bliss. Their only focus was one another and their growing family. Her presence wasn't going to disturb that. Granted they hadn't seen each other in a little over two years, I was certain that Ladi and Ace wouldn't care either way. It was her that I was worried about. Monica knew about their son, Ace Jr., but I wasn't sure how she would react to finding out they were going to have another baby. Monica had an irrational attachment to a man that didn't want her, and she couldn't seem to let it go. From what I could tell, she was attached to the idea of Ace and everything he had to offer. She wasn't attached to Ace the man; she was attached to what she potentially had lost. She tried to conceal it, but I saw right through it.

"Oh ok, just wondering." She fought to keep her smirk from breaking free.

"That's what you wanted to ask me?" I asked confused as to why any of that mattered.

"No, I actually wanted to ask if the guy I'm dating can come?"

"Hell no!" I yelled, answering louder than I attended to.

"Hear me out Angel," she sighed and proceeded to

spew irrelevant information at me, "I want you to meet him. He's a really good guy and he is so fine."

"Fine doesn't get him a pass into my children's party. This isn't about me meeting him Monica." We both knew it wasn't. It was going to be a failed attempt at making Ace jealous. The only person that was going to make uncomfortable was the new guy that she was seeing. He was going to be the one thrown in an awkward situation because Monica was for sure going to put on a show. I was not going let it happen.

"So, Ace gets to bring someone, but I can't?" Her neck moved side to side with each word she spoke.

I didn't understand why it was so hard to comprehend. As if she told a joke, I started snickering. That only irritated her further. Ten years with Saint had taught me a few things and one was to always find humor in other people's stupidity. "First of all, that's his wife not some random that he picked up on the street. Second, if I believed that you wanted to bring him because you didn't have some hidden agenda, then maybe. But I'm not going to watch you act a fool, especially not at my children's birthday party."

"Ok, well can you meet him today and then decide?"

"I'll meet him, but my answer isn't going to change," I responded, closing the issue. We spent the next hour finishing up the minor details for the party.

We ended brunch, with her deciding that it was a good idea for me to meet him sooner than later. The two of us drove our separate cars to her place. Hopefully, this guy was the real deal if she wanted me to meet him that badly. Everyone deserved someone to be theirs and all about them. For that to find Monica, she had to put her focus on herself. When Saint and I first got together, I had to do the same. There was healing that I had to do on my own for us to get to where we were now. I fought him, my heart, my feelings —I fought myself for a week before I was able to open up to the idea of me deserving something good for once in my life. Healing aided in me uncluttering my mind, body, and spirit.

Monica and I made it to her apartment at the same time. She called him right as we made it inside. Twenty minutes into our conversation, the door being unlocked paused our conversation. Maybe it was serious if he had a key to her apartment. A large mocha colored skin man walked through the door. His flashiness was a quick turn off. I was almost blinded by the three diamond chains around his neck. If the chains weren't enough, he had a diamond ring on each finger. It blew my mind to think that someone felt all of that was necessary. Not wanting to make any assumptions, I waited from Monica to introduce us to one another.

He barely got through the door before she was all over him. Monica was extremely short, no taller than five feet tall. She was smaller than me at a size ten, but her hips were almost the width of mine. He had to be no less than a foot taller than her. I watched as he bent down to hug her, his hands groping her behind. He was just about to put his hands underneath her dress when his eyes connected with mine.

He cleared his throat, causing her to look back at me. "My bad Angel," she apologized with the giddiness of a sixteen-year-old falling in love for the first time.

If what I had just witnessed was a sign of what she thought was going to happen at the twins' party, she had lost her damn mind. There was no doubt in my mind that she would do worse the second she saw Ace and Ladi together. That quickly, my answer had changed from hell no to fuck no.

She closed the door behind him but when she went to

grab his hand to pull him towards the couch, he didn't budge. I began feeling uncomfortable as he stared at me. Monica must've noticed because she cleared her throat as she placed her hands on her cocked hips.

Instead of that directing his attention to her, he asked me, "Do we know each other?'

Monica's head whipped around so fast, she could've caught whiplash. "Not at all," I replied.

There was no way that I would've met someone as flashy as he was and not remember. Saint and I always joked about people that had to wear their money and status. It was sign of either insecurity or not knowing how to act after finally getting something. This nigga was probably both.

"Are you sure? We have to know each other. You look too familiar for us not to," he insisted.

Maybe he was a patient of mine from the hospital. I saw too many on the days that I worked there, to remember all of their faces. Just when I was about to answer him Monica said, "She works part-time at Jackson Memorial Hospital as a nurse."

Monica's insecurities were beginning to ooze from her pores to the point where she gave a stranger my work information. In the back of my mind, I knew what she was thinking but she couldn't have been more wrong. Saint was the only man I ever wanted or would ever want. From the day we met, no other man could say that I gave him the time of day. My husband took care of me in a way that I was positive no one else could. The flashy man with a diamond grill, three neck chains, and ten rings didn't hold a candle to my Saint. It wasn't because Saint wasn't ostentatious, but his spirit was welcoming. Saint had a hard exterior but a heart of gold.

"That's not it," he responded without as much as looking away from me. I started getting uncomfortable, desperately wanting to end our encounter.

"No that has to be it. She doesn't go anywhere but work. If she's not there, she's either with me, or her husband, Saint. He owns Chez Saint. Remember? You've seen our pictures together," Monica blurted out, making me want to knock her little as down.

She could've said all of that without giving out my husband's name and his business information. Saint's life before we started our family wasn't something anyone in our family knew about. Ace and I were the only ones. He kept me far away from it. This character seemed sketchy. I hated assuming that but that was the vibe he gave off. My suspicion was confirmed when his eyes enlarged at Saint's name being mentioned.

"So, you're Saint's wife?" He was smirking at me, but his tone was condescending.

"Yes, that's my husband. Do you know him?"

"Nah, I don't. He has a familiar name and you have a familiar face. I'm looking forward to getting to know the both of y'all." He winked at me and smiled, displaying his diamond encrusted grill.

Whoever he was, he was lying. I made a mental note to talk to Saint about it as soon as he came home. He was working late, so I would have to either set my alarm or battle my sleep to stay awake. He rarely woke me up if I was already asleep when he got home late.

Not wanting to stay any longer, I checked my phone as I grabbed my purse to leave. Monica was still standing there, looking back and forth between us. It took her a minute to say, "Why are you leaving? Loco just got here."

Loco? I said to myself. "A text came through. I have to

pick up the babies." I hated lying to her but the uneasy feeling in my stomach was increasing with each second I was in her home. Loco walked past me and went straight to the kitchen, to her refrigerator without as much as saying another word. She left him inside and walked me to my car. We said our goodbyes and parted ways but not prior to me telling her *FUCK NO* to her man attending the twins' party.

*a*ngel
    Saint and I had one nanny that we only used as needed. Neither of us really liked to use her. She was good at her job, but we preferred the children to be around family. More times than not, his mom would be in town and would watch them for us. After Miracle and AJ were born, she started visiting every month. Both of his parents were back in town being that twins party was around the corner.

    She took the liberty of preparing dinner for us while I met with Monica to finalize everything. I was sure it was for Saint because she babied him more than any normal mother should. Our relationship started off rocky when Saint first introduced me to Jolie. Whether it was the age difference or the fact that I was the first woman he introduced to her, she did not like me. After she realized that I loved her first born and wasn't going anywhere, she warmed up to me. She was a very loving woman and it was evident that Saint learned how to love from her. Saint inherited her dark skin and height, but he looked like his father.

    "They've been fed the lunch you left for them. I was

just about to bathe them before you came," Ma said as I sat my purse down on the kitchen counter.

"Thank you for everything, Ma. Saint is not playing about making everything bigger and better than last year."

"That's my boy," she said before putting the pans of food in the oven. She finished putting all four pans in and said, "There's enough food to last until the party, so no cooking for you. Focus on the party, ok." I loved when her St Lucian accent came alive. She was able to make it thick at will and switch it proper within the same sentence.

"Ma, you didn't have to." I gave her a hug to thank her for going out the way for us.

"No problem, Angel. You do a lot. It's ok for me to help when I can."

The acknowledgement and love of a mother figure was something I lacked growing up. Ma gave me a hard time in the beginning but when she gave me her love, she buried me in it. I never resented her for being standoffish towards me in the beginning. When you were protecting the ones you loved, it was only right to do what you had to do. Becoming a wife and mother taught me that.

"Thank you again Ma, you've done plenty. I'll bathe them and you can go enjoy your husband. Tell Pops I said hi."

Following a goodbye hug, she promised to be back to watch the kids the next day and for me to not request the nanny, as she left out. It was my last workday of the week. As much as I loved my job, the twelve-hour shifts were hard to get through some days. Most people didn't understand why I did it when I didn't have to. It wasn't for anyone to understand but Saint and me. He made sure that everything I dreamt about became my reality.

Saint wanted to marry me before he knew about my

legal status. Two months after I joined him in Miami, he proposed making me the happiest woman alive. But initially, I thought he did it out of pity. He proved me wrong when he showed me the receipt for the ring. The date was clear as day. He bought it the morning he dropped me off after our second date. Saint was able to get me a student visa first, so that I was able to study nursing and he paid my way through undergrad. The student visa was easier to get because of the possibility of immigration delaying our process for fraud. I had no record of being in the country, so we didn't want to risk it. Harmony got lucky, there was no saying if luck would be on my side as well. We got married while I had my student visa after which, he applied for my green card. Three years after that, I was able to apply for my citizenship. Saint gave me love, hope, and trust. He said I didn't owe him anything, but I did owe it to myself to cherish every part of the life he gave me. The twelve-hour shifts, the children, himself, and all of the craziness that came along with him.

I left the kitchen and went to the family room. Heaven and Saint Jr. were watching PJ Masks while Miracle took a nap in her playpen.

"Mommy's babies." They stood up and both came running towards me as soon as they heard my voice. I squatted right as they reached me, permitting them to wrap their little arms around my neck. Taking them to the downstairs full bathroom, I undressed them both and sat them in the tub. When they were done with bath time and play time, I dressed them both. Heaven just had to wear a dress and SJ wanted to wear whatever his daddy would wear—basketball shorts and a plain t-shirt.

Afterwards we went back in the family room. I let them watch one more episode of their favorite show while I got

Miracle up to bathe her as well. Once I was done with her, I took them to the kitchen for us to enjoy dinner together, not forgetting to send Saint videos of all three eating to brighten up his workday.

We spent a couple of hours playing the games that they chose after dinner. By nine o'clock, I was exhausted, and it was time to put them to bed. Once there were all down, I took a quick shower and then got in bed myself. Sleep took over me as soon as my head hit the pillow.

———

Waking up to kisses on my midsection, I opened my eyes. Saint's silhouette made its way down to my treasure box. His lips slipped in between my folds, pulling a loud moan out of me. Saint's large tongue twirled around my pearl powerfully and rapidly. Moaning into her as my juices coated his tongue. Pushing my knees up to my chest, Saint entered my waterway using only his tongue as his guide. I was unable to tell where our connection ended or where it began as his tongue maneuvered in and out, in and out, in... and out, I lost all five my senses.

He removed his tongue, giving me a moment to regain my auditory sense only to hear him say, "Fuck my face baby."

He stuck his tongue back deep inside her entryway, signaling me to do as he requested. I positioned my right hand on his smooth bald head and sprang my hips up and down as he murdered her, leaving me defenseless to the orgasm that was milliseconds from taking over my body. Right before I reached the highest level of ecstasy, he replaced it with his finger. He latched onto my pearl, granting me permission to ride the wave of the high his tongue had provided me with. Saint detached himself from me, only to rejoin us at the lips, giving me the pleasure of tasting the molasses that my treasure had fed him and satisfied his late-night craving. Lost in his kiss, lost in him, my hand traveled down to his harden rod.

"Tonight was about you, baby. Wake me up to that in the morning." He gave me one last kiss before he got up from the bed. Saint was still wearing the slacks and dress shirt that he wore to work. Removing his clothes, he disappeared into the bathroom. As he was in the shower, I pondered on how I was going to tell him about my interaction with Loco. It wasn't something I could just keep from him. I had already had one secret, and I was not about to hold another one. The way Loco reacted to his name, told me he knew Saint. How he knew my husband, I wasn't sure. It wasn't a feeling I could write off either. If something was off, chances were, they were off. Saint engrained that in my head every day before he retired five years ago.

Saint emerged from the bathroom with nothing covering his firm body. He told me to wait until the morning, but he was making it hard to. Shaking the adulterated thoughts out of my head, I focused back on the issue of Loco.

"Babe, I need to tell you something," I said. He reacted just as I knew he would. He squinted his eyes at me, climbed into the bed, and enveloped me into his beefy tattoo-filled arms. Saint never verbally told to me proceed. Whenever I said those seven words to him, he responded with those same actions every time.

Instinctively, I laid my head on his chest and asked, "Do you know someone named Loco?"

His body immediately tensed up. "Why?"

Beginning with my conversation with Monica at our

brunch date to my introduction to Loco, I told him everything. His bushy eyebrows furrowed, and his facial expression hardened the more I told him. Based on his reaction, my distrust for Loco was dead on.

"I'll handle it," was all he said before kissing me on the forehead.

Handle it? I needed more than just an *I'll handle it.* "Handle it how?"

"Baby, you know I can't tell you everything when it comes to that part of my life. Just know, if he is how you described him, it's likely that is the Loco I know from my past life. Don't worry, I'll take care of it first thing in the morning. Trust me."

Since the day Saint visited me in Nashville and I fully gave myself to him, I never doubted him. He didn't have to tell me that, I trusted Saint with every fiber of my being. Nothing could ever change that.

CHAPTER 15

*S*aint

Sleep never came last night. As Angel slept, I spent the night going over how to best handle Loco. Based on what Angel told me, I knew it was him. It had been over five years since I last saw him. We ended our business relationship on bad terms. He was demoted for making a mistake. Dice came down at my request and took his place. Loco came highly recommended by my connect at the time. Not knowing anyone in my Miami, I took his recommendation. The only reason I didn't let him go completely was because bitter niggas did bitter nigga shit. I kept him close but at arm's length. The moment I retired and made sure that I could no longer be connected to the game, he's fate was no longer in my hands. Jonas retired soon after I did, leaving Dice and Legend in charge. He was the weak link that we kept around on the strength of the respect I had for my connect. Once I was gone, his place was longer secured. Dice and Legend iced him out. He came to see me when he heard I was opening up Chez Saint, begging me to talk to Legend and Dice for him. It was out of my hands because I had cut all ties with that part of my life. I wouldn't be surprised if that nigga was still harboring hate in his heart because of it.

The first thing I did when morning came, was reach out to Dice. He and I hadn't spoken in years. We had a mutual understanding that as long as he was a part of that life, our contact had to be limited. I didn't want any of it around my children. But I knew he would come through for me and he did just that, by getting me Loco's address.

As I sat in my car, I prayed that the conversation I planned to have with him went well. Loco shouldn't have known what Angel looked like. She was never around that part of my life. I made sure that no one could connect her with me. That's just how far removed she was. Her safety and freedom meant more to me than my own. Whatever it took to keep her out of harm's way, I made sure to do it. Which only meant one of two things. He didn't leave when I told him to leave at the airport ten years ago, or that nigga had been on some creep shit in the past. Either way, it was going to end after he and I had our talk.

Then there was Monica. When I first met her, I was glad that Angel was open to making friends. It was a sign of her progression on learning to trust people. Monica was cool people but then I started feeling like she was taking advantage of Angel. Whenever they went out, Angel always paid. It honestly wouldn't have bothered me if I didn't feel like she expected it every time. Other than that, she was a good friend to Angel and loved my children, so I was cordial with her. As soon as she started dating my brother, my full-blown hatred of her manifested. This situation didn't make it any better because she could've handled it better. She offered up my wife's information to a man that didn't care about her, due to her jealousy. Angel didn't have to tell me that was the reason why. I dealt with women like Monica in the past. She was the worst kind; in it for the money, desperate for attention, and only loyal to herself when it came to men

Once the sun went down, I made my way to his front door. Banging my fist on the door, I waited for him to come open it. Loco had always been arrogant, so I knew he'd come answer. He'd let me in and try to test me. That's what weak men did. They tested men that were more powerful than them. It helped build their confidence. I had more to lose now than I did five years ago, but I was still Saint.

"How did I know that I would be seeing you this soon?" Loco asked right as he opened the door.

Drawing my fist back, I threw a right hook, causing him to stumble backwards into his home and onto the floor. I entered, closing the door behind me. "Because you thought it was appropriate to speak to my wife. You thought it smart to even threaten her, Loco. I really can't be too surprised because you've always been a stupid nigga."

Blood fell from his mouth as he spoke, "I just want my spot back, Saint. That's it. You're the only one that can make that happen."

The name Loco fit him perfectly. He had to be out of his mind to threaten my wife to get in contact with me. I vowed to Angel that she would never encounter fear after the life she lived. If I had to add another body to my five to make it happen, I would. Rage traveled through my veins when I recalled how uncomfortable she felt with his tone and the way he looked at her.

"How do you know my wife?"

"Monica. Monica talks about her all the time. How well off she is and how she has everything. She complains how Angel works when she doesn't have to. She's obsessed with her, man. She'd show me pictures and how they were planning a party. I told her to get me invited, but she said I had to meet Angel first." Most of that wasn't news to me. I didn't doubt that Monica loved Angel, she did. But envy was a sin that made its owner act out of character. That ugly green-eyed monster was a permanent habitant of Monica's heart. He confessed that he stayed at the airport to see who it was that had my head so gone. He knew everything about Angel because Monica told him everything, but Monica was unaware about his connection to me. Then when he saw her, he thought it wise to threaten her to get me to come to him. He couldn't have been more wrong.

"My answer is no." Just as I was done, Legend and Dice came through the door that I made sure to leave unlocked for them. Whatever they chose to do with him, was not on me. That wasn't my life anymore. Angel was my life. She was my strength and my guide through life. I couldn't risk losing all of that over a man that didn't know his place.

After I left his house, I went to pay Monica a visit. We were long overdue for a heart to heart. Changes would have to take place if she wanted to be Angel's friend. Monica lived about twenty minutes from Loco's house. Pulling into the parking lot, I noticed Angel's car. She was supposed to be at work. I began walking full speed towards Monica's apartment. Anger surged through my veins. I didn't mind her calling off work, but I specifically requested that she keep her distance from Monica until I handled the situation with Loco.

The door was slightly open and the two were engaged in a heated argument. Just when I was about to go in, Monica's words halted my step, "You got your tubes tied and didn't tell me, but you told Ladi! I'm your best friend."

"Why were you even going through my phone while I was in the bathroom!" Angel screamed.

I blacked out as I busted through the door. Startled, they both turned around to see me standing at the doorway. "What did you say Monica?"

Monica looked between Angel and I but didn't answer the question. "Baby," Angel whispered, taking a step towards me. I took one back. As much as her love healed any pain I had ever gone through, I was too afraid it wouldn't be able to heal this one.

"Repeat what you said right now!" I barked, causing the two of them to jump back. Tears formed in Angel's eyes, slowly rolling down her pecan colored cheeks. The last time I had seen those tears was after Miracle's birth. The irony of it tormented my soul. Ten years, I put my all into gaining and keeping her trust. I took down every single brick of the wall that she barricaded her heart with. My heart had its own scars from the barbed wire she had surrounding hers to keep love from coming in. I had literally killed for her. A woman that after three encounters, I knew would be my wife. All of that, only for to go back on her word of giving me honesty and trust.

"Please baby, let me explain," she pleaded with her words and tears, but they didn't faze me. I didn't want her to beg. No pleading. None of it. All I wanted were honesty and trust.

"I did it for us baby. Please let me explain. I didn't want us hurting anymore. I regret it baby. I swear I do. I'm going to reverse it, baby. I didn't tell you because I was trying to protect you." With each word she spoke, she took a small step towards me. With each step she took, I took one back.

I didn't like that she did it but a part of me, the important part understood why she did it. She wanted to protect us from pain, I got that. She was afraid of another loss, I understood that, too. My heart didn't understand but logic did. For the first time when it came to Angel, I was going to side with logic instead of my emotions.

"When did you do it, Angel?"

Angel began chewing on the inside of her right cheek and I became numb all over. Her tell. Whatever she was about to tell me, I could already feel the effects the devastation that was going to rain down on me. My chested tighten as I awaited her answer.

"Right after Miracle was delivered."

A year and half. She kept it from me for a year and a half. My already boiling blood grew hotter. Turning away from her, I used every ounce of strength I had left in me to punch a hole in the wall that was next to the doorway. Monica stood there frozen. Angel. My Miss Pecan. The woman that changed my life for the better brought it crashing down with five words. *Right after Miracle was delivered.*

The twins were a natural birth while Miracle was delivered via a c-section. It was a different experience, so I didn't know what to expect. She had the doctor tie her tubes with me in the same room. She didn't value my opinion enough to discuss it with me first. Angel's needs and wants came before mine. If that was something she felt was best for her, I swear I would've gone with it. My soul might've suffered but for her, I would've taken any amount of pain as long as she was happy. As long as her spirit was at peace, I would take one hundred bullets to the head. But to have her do it behind my back and then hide it for over a year, broke me. Ten years later, Angel had finally succeeding in breaking me down. I had no more fight left in me.

"I'm going to walk away," I said. She fell to the ground, sobbing uncontrollably. Monica ran to her side, held on to her, and let her cry in her arms. That had always been my job, but she took away my desire to do it.

"I vowed that I would never raise my voice to you or at you. If I stay here any longer, I'm going to end up breaking that vow." Leaving her on the floor in Monica's embrace as she apologized profusely to me, I walked out.

My mind began racing as soon as I made it to my car. I rested my head on the steering wheel, trying to process everything. Ladi knew but I was sure she didn't tell Ace. He would've told me. Starting up my car, I headed to Ace's house. I couldn't be around Angel. We needed space. I loved my wife more than anything but with the way I was feeling, there was no telling how I would act towards her. It was best I kept my distance for the moment. Even though she broke our vows, I was not going to do the same by disre-specting her.

For a minute, I felt like a hypocrite because I had kept something from her. That quickly went away since the two were not the same. They were gone from this earth for damaging her. She heard me talk about expanding our family and actively trying and knew it wasn't possible. The two secrets were definitely not the same.

CHAPTER 16

A^{ngel} My world turned upside down in a matter of minutes. The image of Saint walking away from me replayed in my head all night. Sleep never visited. One text message was all he sent me. Just one. He didn't come home, and his phone was turned off. Just one text asking me to give him one night of solitude. A night so that he didn't have any anger towards me. No amount of love that I could've given him would be sufficient enough to take away the aching of his heart.

That was never how it was supposed to play out. Towards the end of my shift, I received an emergency call from Monica. Apparently, her and Loco had gotten into a huge fight because she told him he couldn't come to the twins' birthday party. He choked her and left. She was afraid he was going to come back and needed someone. I rushed over there, not even thinking to call Saint. As soon as I made it to her apartment, she apologized for being a subpar friend at times. Monica even apologized for how she acted towards Ladi and Ace. She admitted that she was

envious of my life and couldn't understand why I had everything. She emptied her heart out to me, compelling me to
feel the sincerity in each word. She claimed she had an
epiphany when Loco had his hands wrapped firmly around
her neck.

I stepped away for a few minutes to use the bathroom.
When I made it back, I found Monica engrossed in my
phone. She had seen a text from Ladi, asking when I
planned on telling Saint about getting my tubes tied. Ladi
felt guilty, which I understood. With me wanting to get it
off my chest, I not only shared the secret, but I unknowingly
shared the guilt with her as well. Monica was upset that I
told Ladi and not her. I was upset that she thought it was ok
to touch my phone. And then Saint showed up.

My anger wanted me to blame Monica. Then it turned
my focus to Ladi. But really, I was the only one to blame. I
was the source of my husband's pain once again. The first
time, he didn't walk away. This time he did, and I couldn't
handle it.

I watched the night leave and the morning come. Ma
called to ask if she could have the kids to celebrate since the
twins' birthday was the following day. Sending a silent
thank you to the man above, I agreed to have the children
ready for her to pick up. She came and I did my best to put
on a brave face. As soon as she left, I returned to bed. That
was one thing that Saint and I agreed on when we got
married. Any marital problems were meant to stay between
us. If it was something that required an outside opinion, we
were allowed one person. Ace was his, Harmony was mine.
A lot of times, outside opinions did more harm than good.
Most of the time really, so that was the reason we had that
rule in place. We wouldn't have made it as far as we did,
based on the opinion of others.

As I laid in bed thinking of what I would say to him when we finally had the conversation, the doorbell rang forcing me to get up. His shirt covered my body, but his absence left my soul completely naked. I grabbed his robe from its usual place at the end of the bed. I dragged myself all the way to the front door hoping, it was him but knowing that it wasn't. That's what this situation did to me, it had me hoping for the impossible.

I opened the door only to be disappointed when I came face to face with Ace. Crazy huh? I knew it wasn't going to be him and I was still left disappointed. Not saying anything to him, I walked to the all-white room knowing that he would follow. I grabbed two glasses and a bottle of Saint's Hennessy on the way. I heard Ace close the door with his footsteps not too far behind me. I sat the two glasses on the coffee table and poured each of us a drink. It was ten in the morning but his shirt, robe, his favorite drink, in his favorite place made me feel closer to him.

"You want a drink?" I handed him the glass before taking a seat on the white couch. Saint was the one that decorated the room. It was his quiet space. My only rule was that he didn't drink in it. But I knew he did.

Still standing Ace removed the drink from my hand and said, "No drinking in the all-white room remember?"

"Nigga please, this is the only place you and Saint drink." We both started laughing as we thought about how he and Saint would act like the room was off limits.

"Dang, I didn't think you knew. He thought he was doing it without you knowing."

"Exactly, he thought I didn't know. It was a joke at first but then I started enjoying when he would act like he hadn't done it." My shoulders fell as did my head, "I miss him Ace."

Ace walked over, sat down next to me, and wrapped his arm around my shoulders. "I know sis."

"How is he?"

"Angry and broken." The sadness in his eyes carried over to my heart, knowing that I was the cause of Saint's brokenness. His anger I could handle. It would pass, but I was clueless as how to put him back together again. I had already planned to get my tubes untied but a new baby wasn't going to fix this. I had made a decision in regard to our marriage without his opinion. On top of that, I kept it a secret for over a year. Not to mention, I told Ladi and he heard it from Monica's mouth unexpectanty. I messed up bad.

"He's coming back today, Ang. To be real with you, he wanted to come back last night, but his anger wouldn't let him. We sat up all night, talking to clear his head. I thought Saint would be the one drinking, not you." He chuckled to himself and shook his head.

I honestly didn't know how things would go with Saint. He never yelled at me but that's what I needed right now. I needed him to release his anger onto me because I deserved it. But his love wouldn't let him. He would rather it suffocate him than for it to punish me. Running away wasn't the solution but I understood why he did it.

I shrugged my shoulders and he continued, "He's outside."

I jumped up to rush outside. My glass slipped out of my hand and onto the floor, staining the white fabric fine carpet that covered the floor.

"We been drinking in here for five years and have never dropped anything. How you do it in fifteen minutes?"

His voice. His scent. His sadness. All three pulled my eyes to the door to find Saint standing there. Defeated but there, nonetheless. Ace winked at me and slipped out, without saying a word.

"Baby," I said. Slowly walking over to me, he picked me up bridal style just like when we bought the house five years ago. Saint carried me up the stairs, all the way into our bedroom. He positioned me at the edge of our king size bed, removed his clothes from the day before, and kneeled in front of me.

When I went to say something to him, he stopped me. "Let me go first, babe. I should've done better at handling the situation."

"No baby, you..." I went to interrupt him, but he cut me off. I was the one that betrayed his trust, yet he was the one apologizing, humbling himself in front of me once again.

"Listen to me, Ang. Yes, you were wrong for what you did. But in trying not to break my vows to you, I ended up doing just that. My emotions got the best of me. As your husband, I could've handled them better."

Ten years later, I still didn't know what I did right to deserve Saint. He was rude and irrational at times but when it came to me and our children, he was loving and sincere through all of his actions. He had vowed to never walk away from me no matter what. He had vowed to never let me wake up alone. Since I moved to Miami, he had hadn't broken them. Even with him being heavy in the streets, whenever I woke up, he was at my side.

"No matter what you did to me baby, I shouldn't have done that. I should've been here with you. I'm sorry, Ang." I couldn't hold back the tears after that.

Tears stained my cheeks as he kissed them away. He must've kissed my face one hundred times before anymore refused to come out. The guilt festering inside of me was at an all-time high. It weighed me down more than before as I stared into his beautiful dark eyes. The pain in them plagued my heart, knowing that I was the reason for it. Knowing that my love may not be enough to rid his heart of what I created.

I slid down to the floor, so that we were both kneeling in front of one another. "I'm not sure what I did right in my life to deserve you, but I pray that God continues to bless our union. Do not apologize for walking away last night. You walked away physically but your spirit was with me. You communicated where you were, and you still told me you loved me before turning your phone off. You did nothing wrong. I was wrong. I was so wrong baby. I'm sorry."

My head fell to his chest and I listened to the mellow tempo of his heart beating against his chest. I permitted it to take over me because after one night, I missed it terribly. He didn't have to apologize for walking away because we both needed that time to reflect. I was one hundred percent in the wrong. Not him, me. I was going to take responsibility for what I caused. Saint was a hothead and he never wanted to disrespect me because of it. That was the reason he walked away. He didn't walk away from me, he walked away so that he didn't take his rage out on me. Someway, somehow, I had to fix this between us to rid him of a guilt he shouldn't have had.

He kissed me on the top of my head and said, "I didn't get any sleep last night."

"You want to sleep in it, baby?" I asked into his bare hard chest.

He chuckled and responded, "When have I not wanted to sleep in it?"

I quickly stood up, removed all of my clothes right before I hopped in the bed with my legs wide open. He only had to remove his boxer briefs. "I know we have to talk about this more and we will later baby. But right now, I just need some of the Nyquil in between your legs."

He climbed in between my legs with the tip of his mushroom shaped head at the gateway of his favorite place to escape. We would talk about it later and I would do whatever I had to do to fix what I had broken. But right now, I was going to give him the escape into ecstasy that his body was in need of.

CHAPTER 17

*S*aint

Once again, Angel had allowed her fear to interfere with our progress. I'd been tested a lot through my years on the earth, but no one tested me on the level that Angel did. She was the only person that had that kind of rule over me. The moment I walked away from her after finding out what she had done, I regretted it. I'd be the first person to admit that I was a selfish nigga, but this didn't have anything to do with that. I wanted to stay and argue with her. I wanted to get in her face and hurt her just as much as she destroyed me with her secrecy. The urge to disrespect her due to her deceit, overpowered the love that was reserved only for her. I hated that feeling. So, I left to clear my head. I drove straight to Ace's house. And even though I was upset with her, I texted her letting her know where I was, that I needed solitude, and that I would always love her.

Love was natural. Neither of us had control over that. A lot of times people would mistake it for admiration. Admiration could be earned through a person's actions, but unconditional love didn't go or come at will. It came when it was supposed to. The fact that my anger conquered it for a second, only meant that I had to leave. Getting through the night was hard. I didn't sleep at all. Thankfully Ace and Ladi stayed up and helped me rationalize my thoughts. Ladi's words replayed in my head as I gazed at Angel sleeping in my arms.

"*Saint she was wrong for how she went about it. I don't know her like you do, but I do believe that it was her weird way of protecting you from getting hurt again. Her and I have talked about the miscarriages a few times. They hurt her but watching you be strong while she got the privilege to crumble, wasn't easy for her. The way you two protect and trust each other is unmatched. Have you not ever done anything you knew was wrong to protect her?*"

I'd committed the most immoral of sins to protect her. And I had no plan of telling her about it. Her freedom was too important. Ladi was right, I couldn't let this one mistake she made, break what we had built in ten years together. Nine years of marriage. An eternity of our souls loving each other.

Ace decided he was going to check on her, I went with him with the intentions of waiting in the car. He was supposed to run in check on her and return with an update for me. My spirit was ready to see her, but I didn't think I was strong enough. After fifteen minutes or so, my feet gravitated towards the home that we shared since deciding to start a family five years ago. The moment I saw her, all my anger was cleansed by the aching of her soul. She did hurt me but, in my selfishness, I had done the same to her. It wasn't fair to either of us. The vows that we made nine years ago weren't made to be broken but if somehow, they were, they could be repaired. Our bond. Our love. Our connection. Those were things that no amount of pain could break.

Angel used to let her fear lead her in everything she did in the past, but it changed with me. It hurt me more than anything to know that her fear of hurting me, led her to make that decision on her own. Was I that selfish towards her? Where did I go wrong? Did I do too much by trying to give her every single thing she desired?

"Saint," she called my name with her eyes still closed.

Kissing her softly on the top of her head I responded, "Yes baby."

"Fear didn't make me do it. It wasn't the reason why I kept it from you. My need to protect your heart was. My love for you was. In that moment, I really did think I was doing the right thing for us. I haven't feared anything since the day I chose you to lead me."

Fear and love were two emotions that drove most of our irrational decisions. The two were often mistaken and even at times interchangeable. Love forced us to protect those around us. The fear of losing them had the exact same result. The one we chose to guide us would inevitably win the battle. We had to make the conscious decision to choose love over all. That's what I did the night before. Yes, fear made me walk away but love brought me to where I belonged. Marriage was never meant to be easy and I lived that daily. I was just grateful to have Angel at my side for the journey. This wouldn't break us. Yes, I felt a moment of brokenness, but it didn't only stem from her mistake. It also stemmed from us being apart from one another. The second I was able to realize that, fear vanished, and love took over.

"I love you so much baby. Thank you for saving me."

Angel's eyes popped opened and she raised her head up

to look at me. "Thank you for saving me. Can you please give me a chance to right my wrong? Let me fix this."

She may have thought that I saved her and to an extent I did, but she did way more for me. She gave me a future. Something to look forward to every day when I woke up. Angel gave me my reasons to live. I was no longer living for the moment and taking life for what it had to offer momentarily. The moment she came to my life, she gave me a purpose. She gave me the ability to receive and give love efficiently. My wife saved me by protecting my heart.

It may have seemed crazy to forgive her in one night but when you had nine years of marriage, one night was too long. Until you met someone that was your heart in human form, you'd never understand the power of love, fear, trust, and commitment. There was no pride among us. She admitted she was wrong and asked for a chance to better it. As the man she entrusted with her future, I owed that to her.

"Hell yeah you can, and it better be good, too! I want flowers and everything." She hit me on my chest and started laughing.

"Whatever you want baby," she said after she was able to contain her laughter.

"Let me cancel the twins' birthday party real quick. That way your focus can be all on me the rest of the week."

"Baby don't play about the kids' party like that." Angel scrunched up her face while giving me a side eye.

"Woman, fuck them kids!" Laughter erupted from us both filling the room. That's what marriage was all about, forgiveness and moving forward. I wasn't going to hold anything against her. She would be given the opportunity to right her wrong and I would keep loving her through it.

After we finally got out of the bed at two in the afternoon, we went to pick up the kids from my mom and dad's place that they were renting while in Miami. Don't get me wrong, I loved how much they loved our children, but Angel and I needed a family day with our kids. Instead of pressuring her for a fourth, I was going to continue enjoying the three that we currently shared. Of course, I still wanted my Blessing, but I was going to let Angel make the decision. Whether she got the procedure reversed or decided we were done, she'd have my full support. She'd be out her damn mind to think I wouldn't give my opinion, but the final decision would be hers. I was ok with that. Marriage meant comprise. It was hard for me to do it at times because like I said, I was selfish when I felt that I was in the right. But this wasn't about right or wrong. This was about making the best choice for our relationship and our family.

We took the kids to the park and had a picnic. Whenever we asked SJ where he wanted to go, he looked to Heaven to answer. It made me a proud father because he made sure his sister was happy. He was just like me. The girls were my heart. They were my babies but SJ, he was my rib. He acted just like me and to see him make sure his sister was good at all times, let me know that I was raising him right. Heaven was a diva, but she listened to SJ. Angel may have never peeped it but if Heaven knew SJ didn't like or want to do something, she wouldn't do it. I could tell they looked at everything Angel and I did. Miracle was daddy's baby for sure. The way the twins loved up on her and protected her, brought joy to my heart daily. That was how I wanted to continue raising them. Another baby would be a great addition but we were already complete.

By the time we left the park, the kids said they were hungry again. Angel said that Ma had food for us at the house, but they only wanted "Mommy's tacos". Even

Miracle said no when I asked if she wanted my tacos. Angel wouldn't let me live it down either.

"It's ok babe, I make better tacos than you. That's all."

"Whatever man, they can have your nasty tacos. I'll make my own."

Angel started laughing so hard, I couldn't help but to start laughing as well. Twenty-four hours ago, she was in tears and I was blinded by rage. Twenty-four hours after that, we were enjoying our family. No matter what, I could never lose that. We had to have a serious conversation on how to move forward. It would wait until after dinner, but it had to be had before the day ended. When we made it home, Angel went straight to making tacos for dinner while I got the kids ready for bed. It was a little after seven. By the time she would be done cooking and we had dinner it would be well into nine o'clock.

Just as I entered the dining room with Miracle in my arms and the twins following behind me, Angel was setting the table.

"How many tacos did you fix me baby?" I kissed her full lips before putting Miracle in her highchair. The twins had booster seats, so that they were able to reach the table with ease.

She rolled her eyes and said, "The same amount you always eat babe, six."

I slapped her on her round ass, causing her to jump and squealed. "Say something as if you don't like it," I playfully threatened her.

"She likes it daddy!" both Heaven and Saint Jr yelled at the same time. The smiles on their small round faces pushed their chubby cheeks up. As if she understood, Miracle started giggling and slapping her little hands together. Being able to witness their joy and happiness after the rough night I had, brought so much peace to me. A calmness that I would forever be grateful for.

Dinner was full of laughter and fun. Angel did her thing with the tacos. I ended up eating two on top of the six she had prepared for me. After we got the kids in bed, her and I returned to the dining room to have a conversation that we were both dreading. We both apologized and agreed to move on but there were more things that needed to be discussed for both our sakes.

We sat across from each other, our only connection being the connection of our eyes that refused to let go. Physical contact would only pose a distraction and that was the last thing we needed. She started off the conversation.

"Sorry," She took a deep breath, released it, and continued, "I could say that over and over again but it'll never express how much I regret how I went about doing what I did."

Her chest moved up and down as she tried to gather her thoughts to best convey her message. She chewed on the inside of her right cheek, looked at me with the upmost sincere look and whispered, "Ask me whatever is on your heart and I will answer you truthfully. Through the power of love and words, let me rid your heart of all of the animosity. Give me one last chance to cleanse you the same you cleansed me ten years ago."

Without hesitation I asked her, "Do you trust me?"

She responded in the same manner, without the slightest hint of hesitation, "Yes, more than I trust myself."

"Why is that?"

"Old habits die hard baby. When fear covers me in darkness, you are the light that chases it away."

Each word pierced my soul, but I couldn't let up. We

needed a refresher of how important trust was in our relationship. "Why did you do it?"

"I didn't want us hurting from losing a third child. I didn't want you going through that pain again. At the time it seemed like the right decision for our family."

As much as I wanted to call her selfish, her logic made sense to me. We made selfish decisions for our loved ones all the time. This was no exception. "Do you regret hiding it from me?"

Her head fell to her chest before reconnecting with my eyes. "More than you'll ever know baby. I've regretted it for over a year."

"Then why did you do it?" I threw out question after question. After the conversation ended, I didn't want us to have to go back and ever revisit it again. If we were moving forward, I needed us to truly to move forward. Nothing left unsaid.

"The pain, baby. I didn't want us to experience another loss again," she whined.

I knew that answer already, it was a Segway to my last question. "Why didn't you tell me?"

"Saint, I knew if I told you, even if you didn't want to, you'd go along with it for me. You'd endure the pain for me, and I was too afraid to put you through that. The irony of it all, I still ended up hurting you."

I reflected on everything she said before asking my final question. The answer didn't matter but it had to be asked. "What do you plan to do?"

"I already called to set up the appointment to have reversed. No, I'm not doing it for you. I'm doing for me and for us. If we are meant to have our Blessing, then she will come."

Not needing to hear anything else, I walked over to my

wife, pulled her out of seat, and gave her the most passionate kiss that we both had ever experienced. Our tongues danced to the rhythm of our heartbeats. Our souls were free to love one another with no restrictions. The void that fear and anger created was filled with our love and trust for one another. Silently, I vowed to never make her feel that keeping a secret from me was better than hurting me, while simultaneously begging God that she would never find out about the secret I kept from her.

"Should I punish you or reward you, Ang?"

"Punish me," she quickly responded, and I planned on doing just that.

*a*ngel

The day of Heaven and SJ's party had arrived, and everything was in full swing. All the people that were close to us came to celebrate our babies turning four. They were going to be starting pre-school which was another milestone they were going to reach. I was not ready for that any more than I was ready for them to be four. So to say I was a little emotional, was a bit of an understatement.

"Everything looks good baby." Saint came and sat next to me at one of the few tables that we had arranged in our backyard. Everything and everybody were in a good space.

There was a huge kiddy pool, slide, and the entire back-yard was decorated with PJ Masks decor just like the twins requested. Auntie Marie and Ma prepared all the food of course. The only thing I made were my tacos. Heaven asked for tacos so baby girl got tacos. Saint was a little jealous and it was hilarious. Auntie Marie even brought a date to the party. It was refreshing to see her giddy with the excitement that came with new love. I didn't think I'd ever seen smile as much. Saint's mom and dad were off somewhere acting like they were new to the idea of love as well. If Saint and I could have a piece of what they had, I was certain we would never have anything to worry about. Ashley, on the other hand, had ended things with her new beau because of his inconsistency. She was still in high spirits and enjoying herself. No love could be lost where it was never found.

Monica and I did a great job at putting everything together. We were in a better place. She apologized for going through my phone but a part of me was thankful that she did. If she had never done that, things wouldn't have played out the way they did. I wasn't surprised to hear that her and Loco broke up and she hadn't heard from him since. Monica was one of the first persons to arrive to help decorate and had been on her best behavior. She was cordial with Ace and Ladi but pretty much stayed out of their way.

It wasn't like the two of them would've even noticed. They were in their own little world as newlyweds. It took me back to when I first moved to Miami. Two months in, Saint asked me to be his wife with a ring he bought after our second date. To this day, it was hard to believe. Six months after that we had a small ceremony with the two of us. We had always been protective of each other. We knew what the other meant to each other, so we had to protect that from the outside world.

Harmony and Saint's best friend, Jonas, both flew into town. They were pretending like they didn't see it but there was definitely chemistry between the two. Everyone saw it because Saint asked me what was going on with them. The two of them officially met at a small reception we had after our ceremony ten years ago. They seemed to have gotten along pretty well. Now the two couldn't even be in the same vicinity. It was to the point that if he was sitting at our table, she would get up. If he saw her coming his way, he'd turn away. The two clearly had a story to tell, but it was their story to tell.

To my request, Saint invited Dice to the party. Without him knowing it, he was the one that brought us together. It was only right that he be a part of this. Saint kept him away because of his involvement in the game but I thought it would be ok for special occasions like this one. He sauntered over to us with a drink in his hand.

"Hey Ms. Lady, do you mind if I ask Saint a question real quick?"

Before I could answer, Saint responded, "Ask, nigga. I'm not walking away from my wife for you."

Saint was rude for absolutely no reason, but we all knew what to expect from him. Dice rubbed his hand down his head and asked, "Shorty with the wide hips. Who is she?" His eyes traveled to where Monica was playing with the kids.

"Hell nah," Saint yelled, doubling over in laughter. I sat there, shaking my head at how he was acting. It was kind of funny, but he didn't have to react that way.

"Crazy as hell, that's who she is," he said once he was able to gather himself.

"She's my best friend…" I started but Saint quickly cut me off,

"That will quit her job as soon as you say hi to her. That's all you though, but don't say I didn't warn you man."

Dice laughed it off and walked right up to Monica. "Why did you have to say all of that?" I asked as soon as Dice was out of ear shot.

"Did I lie though?" He started laughing again while I just shook my head at how goofy he was.

Saint said it best, we were a living and breathing contradiction. We were everything that wasn't supposed to be but was meant to be. We would never be the "perfect" fit, but we made sense. Our love wasn't untainted because we weren't. We were both soiled and stained but we helped clean each other up. There was no other love I could envision other than the kind that we had. One where we were able to build up ourselves and build together. A love unrefined. I wouldn't have it any other way.

*S*even months later
        Angel

"This is it, Angel," Ladi announced.

Today was the day that Saint and I were renewing our wedding vows in front of our closest family and friends, to celebrate our ten years of marriage. The night Saint came into my life eleven years ago, he gave me everything that I dreamt of ever having. He afforded me the future that I desperately wanted. The happiness he offered me gave me a glow. The love he poured into me gave me an extra pep in my step. We gave each other purpose. Saint and I didn't live for each other, we lived for ourselves. He lived for him and I lived for me. That allowed us to be able to give ourselves to one another completely. A person that was not whole wouldn't be able to do that. It would be impossible to fully give yourself to someone if you couldn't give yourself all of you. It took me a while to get there but through his patience, I was able to say that I was a whole person before I gave him myself to him.

To celebrate ten years of vowing ourselves to one

another, was unbelievable knowing where I came from. I was lost when we first met. All the potential but no way to build on it. Saint helped me with that. He made sure I got every opportunity that was available to me. If I didn't take it, it was because I didn't want to do it.

After putting the kids to bed the night before the ceremony, while I was in the shower, he got in with me. What I thought would lead to shower sex turned into a conversation that replayed in my head right as I was about to walk out into our backyard, and say I do for the second time. Both our small ceremony and reception were taking place there.

The water poured out the large showerhead, piercing my skin with its warmth. I let it run down my body as I took a moment to reminisce on how far my husband and I had come. The shower door opened, and Saint entered, shutting the door behind him. I turned around and we stood six inches apart from each other. Saint stood next to the bench he had installed in our shower, admiring my body. A body he knew every curve to. A body he spent eleven years exploring. A body that was once considered a debt payer, but he saw as the vessel that held his soul.

"Stop drooling wifey. I'll take care of you in a minute," *he teased me.*

I loved and hated his humor. It made him who it was but sometimes, I wish he did have a filter. "Shut it," *I responded.*

He slowly stepped closer to me and whispered in my ear, "Angel you are everything that I love about this life. Tomorrow we are saying I do again after ten years, it's only right that I ask you what I have to ask you now since I'll probably be too drunk tomorrow."

He let out of a light chuckle and pulled me in tighter. I wasn't sure what he had to ask, but I nodded my head, granting him permission to continue. "The night I met you, I didn't expect to meet anyone let alone my soulmate, but I did. I thought back to when you used to think that you didn't deserved my love, my loyalty, and trust. That you didn't deserve me. I never asked you in the past but before we do this for a second time, just answer this one question for me. Do you know that you deserve me?"

I remembered that conversation like it happened just hours ago. The circumstances of my life led me to believe that I didn't deserve anything good especially if I hadn't earned it. I escaped both of my situations but mentally and emotionally, they had a bondage on my self-worth. Getting my degree, becoming a nurse, marrying Saint, and giving birth to my children were proof that I was deserving of everything I ever wanted.

Achieving my goals and the new-found ability to give and receive love properly from a man that was practically a stranger to me eleven years ago, were proof that I deserved it all. Without any reluctance I answered, "Hell yeah, I'm dope as fuck."

Saint chortled before bringing his lips down to mine. "I swear you are made for me. That response was proof of that."

With one swift movement, he pressed my body against the wall, lifted my leg up, and connected our flesh. I watched as my leaking nectar coated his hardened rod. He left me empty the second he broke our connection, only to fill me up back up with just one thrust...

"Are you nervous?" Ashley asked as she sipped on her bitter ass wine.

Rolling my eyes at her I asked, "Why do you always ask the most obvious questions?"

Her, Harmony, Ladi, and Monica all started laughing before Monica said, "Yeah, you are Saint's wife for real."

The four of them had just gotten done helping me get

dressed in my ivory colored spaghetti strapped Lulu's True Love maxi dress. It was a high-waisted with a full Georgette maxi skirt. The straps and sheer mesh bodice were decorated in rhinestones, sequins, and iridescent beads with a plunging V-cut in the back and a small one in the front. It was simple but elegant. What made it even more special was that Heaven and SJ helped me pick it out. The dress went perfect with my honey brown pixie cut.

It was nice to be able to have them all in the same room and they be able to get along. Ladi and Monica would probably never be best friends, but they were cordial and that was good enough for me. She was all vested in Dice at that moment but who knew how long that would last. They went back and forth so much that I didn't see any real commitment in their future.

"I just wanted to know," she said before guzzling the rest of her wine down.

Monica poured me a shot of Hennessy and I declined it, causing all of them to look at me funny. Saint being drunk was enough for everyone. They didn't need us both drunk. Plus, I needed a clear head for this. Truth was, I was nervous. The renewal of our vows symbolized our new beginning. A beginning that I had no idea where it would lead us to, but I trusted Saint to guide me through.

"I'm ready." They walked out to take their seats. Then the song, *Honesty* by *Pink Sweat$* came on. Tears began forming and I made no attempt to stop them from falling. I had only heard that song once when Saint told me that it reminded him of when we first started dating. The lyrics described the start of our journey perfectly. The door opened to reveal the backyard, and I did my best to not fall over. The transformation of our backyard was breathtaking. Lanterns and hibiscus flowers were all strategically placed all over the backyard. It looked like it came straight out of a magazine.

My eyes shifted to the right and my birth parents-- whom I had only met once since being taken to America at age four--were standing by the opened door, waiting to walk me down the aisle. This was all Saint's doing. It was hard to form a relationship with them over the years after Saint was finally able to locate them in Jacmel, Haiti three years ago. As much as I fought my past, it made it hard to connect with them. But to have the both of them there meant the world to me and I was hopeful for a new beginning with them as well. My dad took my right arm and my mom took my left.

The closer I got to my husband, the stronger I became. He had always been my strength. Ten years of marriage proved that. Saint had the biggest grin on his beautiful, dark chocolate face. The tears from my eyes matched his. He shook his head right as I made it to him. We wiped each other's tears before Saint took my hands into his. With our children at our side, we exchanged our vows to one another. Promising to love, respect, uplift, and most importantly trust one another.

Once we were done, everyone cheered and clapped as we ended our vows with a kiss. I had to literally pull myself away because Saint almost undressed me right there in front of everybody.

"Calm down baby," I said.

"Man fuck these people. Nobody is going to stop me from showing my wife love." I laughed but of course, he was dead serious.

Right after the ceremony, the reception started. It quickly turned into a full out Caribbean party. For the first time, Saint's mom and Auntie Marie didn't ask to cater.

They were too busy enjoying their men to cook for us. Chez Saint catered the food for the reception, and it made me reflect on the growth of my husband. The drug dealer turned restaurant and lounge owner. I, once a restavek, with no clear future turned into a nurse, wife, and mother of...

"Excuse me! Can I get everyone's attention please!" Saint yelled into the mic. "I just want to thank everyone for coming. To my wonderful wife of ten years, I can't believe you agreed to a lifetime with me for a second time."

Every cheered and laughed. They all knew how Saint was, so a few even agreed with him. Taking the mic from him I responded, "You're the one that's stuck with me. There's no leaving me with four kids."

Saint stumbled back while grabbing at his chest. Everyone gasped before yelling congratulations. I had gotten the tubal ligation reversal done a week after we had the final discussion about the situation. We didn't get pregnant immediately afterwards, but I was hopeful. Miracle's pregnancy announcement was done as a surprise to him on my birthday, so I wanted to do same thing with this one.

Saint came closer and placed his right hand on my stomach. "For real?"

"For real. I'm twenty weeks and we are getting our Blessing."

Saint called it. We were having another girl. He and I had discussed that if I were to get pregnant then I could get my tubes tied again after delivering but I wasn't sure if I wanted to. After the birth of our little girl, then we would make that decision together.

"I love you, Angel Baptiste."

"I love you, Saint Baptiste."

He offered me a soft kissed, pulled away, and said, "Forget this party, we need to celebrate this in private."

After talking to a few people, we snuck out of our own avowal renewal reception, so that he could reward me. Our love was never meant to be cookie cutter because that wasn't who we are as individuals. But I wouldn't change it for anything. We were two tainted people that found love in one another and that was a love unrefined.

The New Beginning

CPSIA information can be obtained
at www.ICGtesting.com
Printed in the USA
LVHW021537061120
670969LV00010B/1104

9 781697 827323